Jessa felt Garrett's gaze on her as she and Hunter came downstairs.

He poured himself a cup of black coffee and carried it to the table. He smiled at Hunter. "Sleep well?"

The boy nodded and dropped his gaze to his plate. Garrett turned his blue eyes on Jessa. "He's a quiet one."

"Yes. Yes, he is."

"How about you?"

She felt a bit off-balance around Garrett, which seemed understandable since he'd literally shaken her off a ladder—and into his arms—the moment they'd met. "Um, am I quiet?"

Garrett smiled again. "Actually, I was wondering if you'd slept well, too."

"Oh. I did, yes. Thank you."

What was it about him that made her feel as if she had to be on high alert? And how could she want to run in the opposite direction yet sit here and take in every detail about him?

The man was a puzzle. One she dared not attempt to solve.

Books by Arlene James

Love Inspired

*The Perfect Wedding
*An Old-Fashioned Love
*A Wife Worth Waiting For
*With Baby in Mind
The Heart's Voice
To Heal a Heart
Deck the Halls
A Family to Share
Butterfly Summer
A Love So Strong
When Love Comes Home
A Mommy in Mind
**His Small-Town Girl

**Her Small-Town Hero
**Their Small-Town Love
†Anna Meets Her Match
†A Match Made in Texas
A Mother's Gift
  "Dreaming of a Family"
†Baby Makes a Match
†An Unlikely Match
The Sheriff's Runaway Bride
†Second Chance Match

*Everyday Miracles
**Eden, OK
†Chatam House

ARLENE JAMES

says, "Camp meetings, mission work and church attendance permeate my Oklahoma childhood memories. It was a golden time, which sustains me yet. However, only as a young widowed mother did I truly begin growing in my personal relationship with the Lord. Through adversity He has blessed me in countless ways, one of which is a second marriage so loving and romantic it still feels like courtship!"

After thirty-three years in Texas, Arlene James now resides in Bella Vista, Arkansas, with her beloved husband. Even after seventy-five novels, her need to write is greater than ever, a fact that frankly amazes her, as she's been at it since the eighth grade. She loves to hear from readers, and can be reached via her website, www.arlenejames.com.

Second Chance Match
Arlene James

Love Inspired

Recycling programs
for this product may
not exist in your area.

 LOVE INSPIRED BOOKS

ISBN-13: 978-0-373-87723-2

SECOND CHANCE MATCH

Copyright © 2012 by Deborah Rather

www.LoveInspiredBooks.com

Printed in U.S.A.

Do not be afraid, little flock, for your Father has been pleased to give you the kingdom.
—*Luke* 12:32

Thanks to my editor, Melissa Endlich, for the time, the attention, the expertise and the inspiration. God bless you, dear lady.

DAR

Chapter One

The dream that had sustained Garrett Willows throughout the dark years of his life was at last about to become a reality. Turning in a wide circle, Garrett sucked in a deep breath, reveling in the sweet, clean greenness of April in Texas. He smiled at the rugged outbuildings and elegant old Victorian house that would become his home and business. Surely, God had created no more perfect of a place for him to open his plant nursery. His bright blue eyes twinkled with delight as he dropped his gaze on the older woman at his side.

"Let's take a look inside," his companion encouraged eagerly. Magnolia Chatam, one of triplet sisters in their mid-seventies, had long been his personal champion. Small and wizened, with her ubiquitous iron-gray braid hanging over one shoulder, she smiled up at him, her curious amber eyes sparkling. "Kent says the repairs are essentially done."

When the Monroe house had suffered fire damage a few months ago, Kent Monroe and his granddaughter, Ellie, had moved into Chatam House, the lovely old antebellum mansion owned by Magnolia and her sisters, until the insurance could be collected and repairs made. No one had been surprised by that particular turn of events. The Chatam sisters were constantly taking in those in need of shelter. What came afterward had surprised everyone, though—and opened the door to the future for Garrett.

He nodded his inky head and, pulling the key from a pocket, let Magnolia in through the back of the house. Wordlessly, they wandered across the back parlor to a pair of doors at the end of the sizable room. According to Kent, one door would open into a short hallway that skirted the dining room, and the other would lead into the kitchen.

Choosing a door, Garrett pulled it open then drew up short. An orange metal ladder blocked the way. Assuming that the workmen had left it there, Garrett placed a hand on each of the nearest metal legs and lifted the ladder to set it aside, finding it surprisingly heavy.

"Wow," he began, clumsily moving the thing only a couple feet. It rocked. And shrieked. Managing to crowd into the small room, Garrett glanced upward in time to see a body falling toward him in a flurry of flailing limbs. "Whoa!"

Heart hammering, Garrett threw out his arms and somehow managed to catch the fellow—or child, given the slight weight—while the ladder stuttered backward.

But what would a child be doing up on that ladder?

No, not a child, he thought, catching sight of the flushed face of a young woman. A very lovely young woman with long, wheat-brown hair tumbling over his arm.

For a stunned moment, Garrett could do nothing more than gape, taking in the triangular face with a dainty nose and big, very dark brown eyes, loosely framed by wisps of straight, golden-brown hair. The slight woman in his arms could not be called beautiful in the classical sense; her face was too unusual for that. But something more than mere shock made Garrett's heart race. Something about that clean, almost angular face seemed both breathtakingly fresh and oddly, achingly familiar, as if he ought to know her. Yet, he was sure that they had never met.

Suddenly those deep brown eyes darkened to black, the generous lips pulled down in a frown, and a sharp elbow jabbed into his ribs as she began to struggle. Garrett swiftly set her on her feet, aware of Magnolia crowding close behind him. The tiny woman glared at him, her dark eyes sweeping over him accusingly as her dainty hands tugged at the hem of her heather-gray T-shirt. One hand crept up to smooth over the weighty mass of her hair before jerking away again. Garrett doubted that she stood as tall as five feet.

"You could've killed me!"

"Sorry. I—I didn't realize anyone—"

"Who are you," she interrupted, "and what are you doing here?"

Garrett shook his head, trying to marshal his thoughts, and belatedly stuck out his hand. "Garrett. Willows. And, um…this is my new house."

"*Your* house?" She backed up, bumping into the ladder, which rocked precariously before settling once more.

"I'm moving in here and opening a plant nursery."

Her big, dark eyes widened even further. "This is *my* house! *I'm* moving in and opening a shop. I made arrangements with the owner this morning."

Garrett matched her frown with his. "That's impossible. I spoke to Kent not four hours ago."

"Kent? Who's Kent?"

"Kent Monroe."

The woman shook her head, catching the butterfly clip that her fall had dislodged from her hair as it flew to one side. Garrett saw for the first time that her T-shirt and baggy jeans were flecked with bits of paper.

"I made arrangements with Ellie Monroe," she declared.

A sick feeling roiled in Garrett's stomach. As Kent's granddaughter, Ellie was co-owner of the house. Moreover, Kent tended to indulge Ellie. If Ellie wanted this woman to have the house, chances were that she would. Garrett felt his optimism drain away. So much for his dreams.

Taking a deep breath, Garrett traded worried looks with Magnolia, who stepped up and said sweetly, "I'm Magnolia Chatam. What's your name, dear?"

The other woman fidgeted for a moment. Finally, she mumbled, "Jessa Lynn Pagett."

"And when did you speak with Ellie?" Magnolia asked.

She shrugged and twisted up her hair, making a long rope of it and coiling it at the nape of her neck before securing it with the hairclip. Long, tendrils of it fell free, wafting about her face. "I don't know exactly. Sometime between nine-fifteen and ten o'clock this morning. She had a break in her class schedule and told us to come over to the school."

"Us?" Magnolia queried with an innocent smile.

Jessa Lynn Pagett's dark eyes darted to one side. "My friend, Abby Stringer, my son and me."

At first glance, she hadn't looked old enough to be a mother, but on closer study, Garrett realized that she could be in her early twenties. He noted that she hadn't mentioned a husband, so he did it for her. "What about your husband? Didn't he want to be with you when you spoke to Ellie?"

"I'm divorced," Jessa Lynn Pagett told him sharply.

More pleased by that information than he should be, Garrett shifted his gaze away and caught a speaking glance from Magnolia. He cleared his throat.

"I know Abby," Magnolia said conversationally, shifting her attention back to Jessa. "When she retired, Ellie took her place teaching at the elementary school."

That connection made Jessa Pagett's story entirely credible. Sighing, Garrett pinched the bridge of his nose between his thumb and forefinger.

"So you arranged to rent the place from Ellie," he said to

Jessa, "and I arranged to lease it from her grandfather, Kent. On the very same morning. Swell."

"All I know," Jessa declared, folding her arms, "is that my son and I are moving in here tonight and I'm opening a shop in the front room as soon as possible."

Biting back a groan, Garrett glanced at Magnolia. She had been instrumental in convincing Kent Monroe to have the place re-zoned residential/commercial recently, with Garrett in mind. Neither of them had considered the possibility that the new zoning would attract others with similar goals to his.

"You've signed papers, then?" Garrett asked dully. That would definitely give Jessa Lynn Pagett precedence as Kent had suggested that Garrett could sign his lease on Friday, two days from now.

Jessa blanched, giving Garrett a glimmer of hope. "The papers weren't drawn up yet. But Ellie said we could go ahead and stay here tonight because—" She broke off, biting her lip.

"Because you have nowhere else to go?" Magnolia surmised gently.

Jessa looked away, swallowing.

"Do you?" Garrett asked, fairly sure where Magnolia was going with this. "Do you have somewhere else to stay?"

Jessa lifted her chin. "Not exactly."

Garrett looked to Magnolia, thinking of something that he'd heard said recently by her nephew, Asher Chatam, an attorney and the fiancé of Ellie Monroe.

"Possession," the astute counselor had declared, *"is nine-tenths of the law."*

In other words, if neither he nor Jessa had signed papers, the one actually in residence could have the upper hand.

Thankfully, Magnolia did exactly what Garrett expected her to do. "Until this is settled," she said kindly, stroking her cleft chin, "you and your son should, perhaps, stay with my sisters and me at Chatam House."

Jessa turned a startled gaze on the older woman. "Chatam House. That's the mansion we passed on the way here. Abby pointed it out."

Magnolia waved away the description. "It's just a big old house with a great deal of room."

A big old house with a ballroom, library, sunroom and more than a dozen bedrooms, Garrett thought wryly. It was the largest house in the entire town of Buffalo Creek, Texas, and had been since before the Civil War.

Jessa shook her head, saying to Magnolia, "We couldn't impose on you like that."

"No imposition at all," Magnolia told her. "You would be entirely welcome, I assure you. We're used to unexpected guests. We delight in them, in fact. Ellie is staying at Chatam House, you know, along with her grandfather."

That ignited a light in Jessa Lynn Pagett's dark eyes. "The Monroes are staying at Chatam House?"

"That's right, and I'm sure that as soon as we get everyone together, we can settle this whole thing," Magnolia told her, folding her gnarled hands against the waistband of her old-fashioned shirtwaist dress. "Though not tonight. I know for a fact that Ellie has a date tonight with her fiancé, my nephew, Asher."

Jessa chewed her full lower lip, digesting this information. "I see. So, it would be for just one night?"

Magnolia smiled, saying, "That's up to you, dear. You can stay as long as necessary. No one will mind."

Looking around her, Jessa considered. Garrett's gaze followed hers. Flakes of scorched, yellowed paper that she'd obviously been peeling off the wall littered every surface from the painted counters and shelves to the hardwood floors. She might be small, but she was obviously capable and had been very busy here. He found that oddly attractive. In fact, he found *her* oddly attractive, which was no doubt a very bad idea.

They were essentially opponents here, each claiming rights to the same property. Attraction could only get in the way. Yet, something about her called to him. Not that a woman like her would ever give a second look to someone like him.

Suddenly, what had, not many minutes before, seemed so sweetly straightforward had somehow become a tangled, confusing mess. And wasn't that the story of his life?

Oh, Lord, he asked silently, *why can't it ever be simple with me?*

Finally, Jessa Pagett nodded. "All right. I accept your invitation. We'll try not to be any bother."

"I'm sure you won't be," Magnolia replied politely, while Garrett tried mightily to believe it. "Honestly, Chatam House is the next best thing to a hotel these days."

"Thank you for the invitation. I—I'll have Abby drop us off later."

Magnolia gave her hands a clap. "Lovely. My sisters and I will look forward to hosting you. And say hello to Abby for me, won't you?" Jessa nodded stiffly. "We'll let ourselves out now and see you later, then." She started away, snagging Garrett by the short sleeve of his faded red T-shirt.

Blinking, he realized that he'd been staring at Jessa Lynn Pagett for some time. He cleared his throat. "Sorry about…" He waved a hand at the ladder.

Her dainty fingers fluttered nervously at her sides, then she shrugged. "Scared me, but no harm done, I guess."

He backed away, saying, "I trust you can lock up."

She gave him a wry smile. "I have a key."

Slipping his from the pocket of his jeans, he held it aloft. "Me, too."

And that about summed up the situation. They both had a claim to the place. The only question now was: Whose claim would actually prevail?

Garrett turned and followed Magnolia from the house. He carefully locked the door behind him and once more pocketed the key, his shoulders slumping.

"Now, now," Magnolia assured him, "all will be well, never you fear."

"I know," he told her glumly, stooping to accept her wiry hug. "I know."

Somehow, it would all work out. If the April afternoon no longer seemed quite as bright as it had earlier, well, it was still a far cry from the darkness of his past.

Thank You, Lord, he prayed silently, tamping down his disappointment and qualms, *for bringing dear old Mags and her sisters into my and Bethany's lives.*

His younger sister, Bethany, had married another Chatam nephew, Chandler, last summer, and together they were raising a young son on their ranch outside of Stephenville, about three hours away.

Whatever happens, Garrett went on determinedly, *I am blessed. Help me to remember that. Always.*

He had the feeling that he was going to need reminders in the days to come.

"I should've known," Jessa muttered, swiping at the hot tears that rolled down her cheeks. Closing her eyes, she turned her face upward, speaking through her teeth, "But just once couldn't it have been easy? Please, God. How can You let this happen now? Is a safe place in this world too much to ask?"

She'd thought that she and Hunter were finally going to get their lives together, but no. That Willows guy thought this was *his* house. And maybe it was. Talk about your major complications.

If that wasn't bad enough, why did he have to be so good-looking, too? The last thing she needed in her life was another handsome man, especially one with electric blue eyes—and a claim on *her* property. This house here on Charter Street was the perfect place for her to open her florist shop and make a home for Hunter. For a couple hours, she'd thought God had answered her prayers, only to have her hopes dashed.

"Well, what else is new?" she asked herself, scrubbing away fresh tears. It wasn't as if God had ever really listened to her, after all.

At least she and Hunter had a place to spend the night. They'd already overstayed their welcome at Abby's retirement complex, which restricted guests to visits no longer than four nights in a row.

Jessa shuddered to think what they'd have done without Abby, who was an old friend of her mom's. When Jessa had finally gathered the courage to leave behind her old life and rebuild here in Buffalo Creek, Abby had not only offered temporary sanctuary, she'd come after them in her old car. She had even thought of the Monroe place for them, having seen a change of zoning notice in the local newspaper. Her personal connection with Ellie Monroe had made the idea seem heaven-sent. Jessa had reached an agreement with Ellie about leasing the place even before she'd seen inside the house, but as soon as she'd walked through the front door, a sense of well-being had come over her, a feeling of home.

So much for that.

Not that she would just roll over and give up. She'd fought fiercer battles, after all. No, she was going to stay, at least for the night, at Chatam House. With the Monroes. And find a way to plead her case. The worst that could happen was that she'd get her money back, some of it, anyway.

Sighing, she dropped her head into her hands. Oh, why, had she let herself spend hard-earned cash on ladders and such to fix up the house, a house that might not even be hers? She groaned aloud, thinking of the business license for which she'd applied that very day. Why couldn't she have waited until the papers on the house had been signed?

The pounding of small feet on bare hardwood jerked her from her pit of regret. She rubbed her face with her hands and put on a smile just as her six-year-old son, Hunter, burst into the room from the kitchen, his shaggy, nut-brown hair flopping.

"Mommy! Abby teached me my lessons already."

"Taught, not teached," Jessa corrected, opening her arms. Hunter collided with her in a glancing hug. "Wasn't that nice of Abby to take over your schooling for the day?"

"Uh-huh," Hunter replied absently. He seemed much more interested in the bits of paper littering the place, dragging the toes of his canvas shoes through them. "It snowed."

Jessa chuckled. "Kind of. Unfortunately, this snow won't melt. It has to be swept up."

Abby appeared in the doorway. She glanced around, remarking, "I see you've made some progress."

"That's what I thought," Jessa told her glumly. Pointing Hunter toward the kitchen and the laundry room beyond, she instructed the boy to see if he could find the broom and dustpan. He ran off to do so, giving Jessa the chance to inform Abby of the mix-up with the house.

"Good grief," Abby commented, the wrinkles in her square face deepening as she considered the situation. She ran a hand over her short, thin, salt-and-pepper hair. "What are you going to do?"

"We've been invited to stay at Chatam House," Jessa said,

reaching out for the broom as Hunter ran up, dragging it behind him.

"Chatam House!" Abby exclaimed. "By whom?"

"Magnolia Chatam. She said to tell you hello."

Abby's thin eyebrows lifted upward, creating a series of grooves in her forehead. "Magnolia is one of the Chatam triplets. We worked together on a panel for the Historical Society."

Jessa had heard all about the Historical Society. With some three hundred buildings of historical significance in town, the society wielded a good bit of influence.

"And who is the man again," Abby asked, "the one who says this is his house?"

That moment when Garrett Willows had caught her in his arms swept over Jessa. She'd been perched near the top of the ladder, reaching for a long strip of paper that dangled just above her head, and the next thing she'd known the ladder had rocked and she'd been falling. Then suddenly a pair of strong arms had caught her and pulled her safely against a broad, rock-hard chest. She'd felt his heart racing in tandem with hers, and though all fear had swiftly passed, she'd felt an insane urge to loop her arms around his neck. A pleased smile had hovered over her lips as she'd gazed up into his handsome face, and then she had realized that he had made her fall and her good sense had, thankfully, come rushing back. Mortified, she'd scrambled out of his arms and tried to catch her breath.

Jessa shrugged, as if he hadn't made much of an impression on her. "Garrett something-or-other." Abby shook her head, so Jessa went on. "Tallish." Six feet, at least, maybe an inch or two over. "Black hair." Thick, coal-black hair that shadowed his square jaws and made his bright blue eyes all the more piercing.

She shivered. Men that handsome always disturbed her.

This one…something about this one frightened her, and it wasn't just his claim on her home. It was more an odd sense of familiarity coupled with instant attraction.

"Hmm," Abby mused, "could be another nephew. There are too many Chatams to shake a stick at, and not just around here, either." She straightened. A busty woman with skinny legs, she wore a boxy shirt and shorts that displayed bony knees. "Well, it's all for the good. After a few days at Chatam House, you and Hunter can return to me. That will give us at least a week to find another place for you."

"In other words," Jessa said morosely, "you think he's going to get this place."

Abby opened her mouth as if to deny it, but in the end, she merely sighed. Jessa figured she was right, but she pushed her hopelessness aside.

No. Not this time.

She had a verbal agreement with Ellie Monroe, entered into in good faith. Money had changed hands. Not much of it, granted, but money, nonetheless. She had invested in the place already and started scraping off the nasty, stained wallpaper in the butler's pantry that was so perfect for her purposes. She had every right to this property, and she would not stand by while some man took their home from her and her son. Not again.

Not ever again.

Meanwhile, she would plan how best to approach this matter. Looking down at herself, she grimaced. She could start by putting her best foot forward. She hoped Abby had an iron.

As usual, the tea tray had been prepared while Garrett and the Chatam sisters attended the midweek meeting at the Downtown Bible Church that evening. Hilda, the cook, poured hot water into the silver pot before Garrett carried the tray from the kitchen. Despite the mouthwatering aroma of Hilda's famous ginger muffins, Garrett felt in a grim mood. Jessa Pagett and her son should have arrived hours ago, but Hilda reported seeing "neither hide nor hair" of their expected guests thus far. Had she decided to stay at the house on Charter Street, after all? He didn't suppose it mattered, in the end. She was bound to get the place if that's what Ellie wanted.

Reaching the elegant foyer, he skirted the sweeping, marble staircase and turned into the large, antique-filled front parlor. It tickled him to see Odelia Chatam cuddled up on the settee with Kent Monroe while Mags and Hypatia pretended not to notice from the wing chairs placed around the low, piecrust table.

The Chatam sisters, maiden ladies in their mid-seventies, were as different as triplets could possibly be. Hypatia was all silver and silk, as regal as a queen. Odelia could not have been more endearing in her flamboyant costumes and oversize jewelry, her hair a soft, wild cap of white curls. Kent obviously adored her, but her many nieces and nephews didn't call her Auntie Od for nothing. Magnolia, on the other hand, his own dear Mags, brought to mind visions of garden spades. Tough and no-nonsense in her funky galoshes and shirtwaist dresses, she possessed a heart of pure gold. As did they all.

"Here we are," Hypatia said, turning as Garrett carried the heavy tray to the table.

"Tea is served," Garrett announced unnecessarily, his words punctuated by the sound of the brass knocker on the front door.

"Our new guests have arrived," Hypatia concluded, as Magnolia moved briskly toward the foyer.

"About time," Garrett muttered. Aware that his heartbeat had sped up, he slowly straightened and turned toward the open, doublewide pocket door, parking his hands on his hips just below belt level.

Several seconds of muted conversation ensued before Magnolia reappeared with Jessa Pagett and a young boy in tow. Mags made short work of the introductions.

"Allow me to make known to you my sisters, Hypatia and Odelia. Garrett you've met. And this…" She waved a hand at Kent, who was even then lumbering to his feet. "Is Kent Monroe. Everyone, this is Jessa Lynn Pagett and her son, Hunter."

Jessa had changed into crisp, dark slacks, a tailored, off-white blouse and dress shoes with tall heels. Wisps of light golden-brown hair framed her face, the mass of it having been twisted up in the back. She smiled and nodded, but he felt her wariness.

The shaggy-haired little boy with her looked to be about four years old and seemed equally curious and uneasy. His plump-cheeked face showed nothing in common with his mother's triangular one, but his dark, troubled eyes were miniature versions of hers. In his baggy jeans and yellow plaid shirt, he looked like someone Garrett had used to know.

Himself. After his dad had died.

Garrett's heart turned over in his chest. There were other houses, he told himself. And this would not be the first or the last time that he suffered disappointment.

Chapter Two

"Won't you join us?" Hypatia asked from her chair, but Jessa shook her head.

"Oh, no. Thank you. We wouldn't want to intrude, and it's been an eventful day." She glanced at Garrett, adding, "We're both tired."

A gentleman of the old school, Kent straightened his bowtie before smoothing the hang of his tweedy sport coat over his prodigious belly and clearing his throat. "My apologies, ma'am, concerning the situation on Charter Street."

Jessa nodded and offered him a strained smile, her gaze again flitting to Garrett.

"Well, it will all be sorted soon enough," Magnolia said, "once Ellie and Asher have a moment to get together with everyone."

After seeing the boy, Garrett figured he knew just how it would all sort out.

"Bad timing," Odelia opined, smiling at Jessa, "with the weddings and all."

Garrett could almost see Jessa Pagett's ears perk up at that.

"Weddings?" she echoed.

"Oh, my, yes," Kent said with a chuckle. "First Asher and Ellie's. Then ours." Reaching down, he took Odelia's hand in his and bent over it, so far as his prodigious belly would allow, to press a kiss to her knuckles. She chirped like a tree full of magpies. This, in turn, set her earrings aquiver, huge clumps of yellow beads to complement the layers of lemony gauze that she wore belted at her waist with a twist of gold rope.

Garrett smiled in sheer delight. They were just so happy, and why shouldn't they be? At their ages, they had put aside the mundane cares that burdened most marriages and looked forward simply to spending the rest of their days together. Odelia was in alt over being a June bride, and Kent was in alt over her, his lost love restored to him after fifty years. Garrett envied them, but at least he enjoyed watching them make calf's eyes at each other. He could hardly bear to be in the same room with Ellie Monroe and Asher. The two of them together made him feel…lonely. For some reason, his gaze went to Jessa Lynn Pagett, who stood staring at the toes of her shoes.

The sisters traded looks, then Magnolia said, "Well, we won't keep you. Garrett, would you mind showing Jessa and Hunter to their rooms? Chester's already taken their luggage up to the small suite."

"My pleasure," he murmured, moving toward the door.

The boy reached for the reassurance of his mother's small hand, shrinking back as if literally frightened of Garrett. Garrett had seen that reaction before, and he did not like what it implied. Carefully, he signaled for mother and son to precede him toward the stairs.

They climbed the wide, tall spiral of gold marble and mahogany with all the enthusiasm of condemned prisoners. Following behind them, Garrett felt a bit offended on behalf of the Chatam sisters, who were the most generous Christian women he had ever met. If he could never quite bring himself to impose upon their kindness more than he must, well, that was to be expected. He was hired help around here, after all, and his gratitude for that fact would not allow him to forget it, even if his sister had married into the family.

Soon, he vowed, he would not even be a Chatam employee. One way or another, he *would* start his business. However, after seeing Hunter Pagett, Garrett could not in good conscience deny that boy a home.

So be it. If God meant the Monroe place for the Pagetts, then He would surely have another place for Garrett.

But when?

"Seriously?" Jessa muttered, emerging from the second bedroom to look around the sitting room. She'd expected a single bedroom with a trundle for Hunter, maybe two connected bedrooms with a bath nearby. This suite of rooms was twice the size of Abby's apartment! If it had a kitchen, it would equal the house in which she'd grown up. She wouldn't think of the house that Wayne had insisted on taking in the divorce. It had always meant more to him than to her.

"I beg your pardon?" Garrett Willows said.

Jessa turned, smiled wanly and waved a hand. "I—I didn't expect this." She glanced around once more, taking in the tasteful cream-and-cocoa décor. The furnishings were a mixture of antiques and modern comfort. A flat-screen TV hung above the fireplace, and Hunter was even now standing in front of it with his mouth hanging open. "It's too much, frankly."

"Yeah, I know what you mean," Garrett conceded with a crooked smile. "And this is the small suite, meaning that it's the smallest in the house. You have to admit, it's much smaller than the Monroe place."

Jessa couldn't argue with that. "I guess I'm just a bit… bewildered."

"Well, that makes two of us," Garrett returned. "It's been quite a day, frankly."

"You can say that again," Jessa muttered, glancing around once more.

"It's been quite a day," Garrett repeated a shade louder than the first time. That elicited a reluctant smile from her.

"I didn't mean that you should literally repeat it."

"I know." He gave her a cheeky grin. "Couldn't resist, though."

A chuckle escaped her, and he gave her a genuine smile, obviously pleased to have lightened the mood.

Oh, this could be dangerous, she thought, forcing the delight from her face.

"Make yourselves comfortable," he advised, pretending not to notice, "and don't hesitate to ask for anything you need."

"We'll be fine," she said blandly. "Thanks for the help, but don't let us keep you."

Apparently, he was in no mood to be dismissed, however. He narrowed his eyes and folded his arms.

"If you decide you'd like a little bedtime snack, the kitchen is downstairs at the back of the house," he informed her. "Hilda keeps the pantry well stocked. Oh, and there's a dumbwaiter down the hall so you don't have to carry heavy trays up and down the stairs."

"A dumbwaiter," she echoed.

"I can show you how to operate it, if you want," he offered.

"That won't be necessary," she replied tersely.

He shrugged. "See you in the morning, then."

"Y-you're staying here?" she asked. She'd been dismayed to find him in the living room with the Chatams. Clearly, he was close to them somehow, but she'd hoped that he wouldn't be staying. She couldn't very well plead her case in front of him, after all. It was bad enough that she'd wasted her best outfit, but now to find that she wasn't about to be rid of him, well, it was enough to make a girl testy.

"Not *here* here," he said, pointing at the floor. "I live in the carriage house." Great. So, was he renting? Family? Freeloading? She was dying to know.

He turned to go, then abruptly spun back to face her. "Oh, um, I should point out that there is some construction going on across the landing. Odelia and Kent are reconfiguring some single rooms into a private suite of their own, but you know how it is with old houses. It takes forever to make changes. Shouldn't disturb you too much."

"About those weddings," Jessa ventured quickly, stepping forward. "I'm a little confused."

"It's very simple," Garrett said with a grin. "Asher Chatam and Ellie Monroe will wed on the fourth Thursday of May, and Odelia and Kent will marry on the fourth Tuesday of June."

"I see."

He chuckled. "I know what you're thinking. A June bride at Odelia's age. It tickles me every time I think about it."

She had been surprised to find that the elderly pair were engaged to marry, but her mother had designed arrangements for more than one such wedding at a local nursing home. Jessa's concerns, however, featured flowers—and work.

"Actually, I was just wondering what florist they're using." She prayed that she didn't sound greedy, but after finding Garrett Willows in the parlor with the family and learning that he lived on the premises, she very much doubted that she would ever claim the Monroe place, let alone open a business there. Maybe she could get a temporary job with the shop lucky enough to garner a Chatam wedding, though.

Garrett snorted and shook his head. "Florist? They don't have a florist. Both couples only became engaged a couple weeks ago and neither is willing to wait too long. That's why the weddings will take place on weeknights. All the weekends were taken already at the church. And, of course, it being the wedding season, all the local florists are booked solid. Between you and me, more than one offered to work in the Chatams, but the ladies wouldn't allow that."

"Why not?" Jessa asked. Her mother had often worked in favorite customers.

"They truly would not want to risk creating hardship for others," Garrett divulged, "but mostly they wouldn't want anyone to think that they were taking advantage of the Chatam name. So, Magnolia will be handling the flowers." He shrugged as if to say she'd do her best.

Jessa blinked. "Magnolia?"

"She does all the flower arranging around the house, and she's been reading about bouquets and corsages and such. There are some wonderful books in the library, by the way, if you're interested."

"Thank you," Jessa returned automatically, her heart beginning to pound. "M-maybe I could help, though. With the flowers. It just so happens that I am a florist. I—I've handled quite a few weddings, actually." Three, to be precise, but she'd helped her mom with designs for many more, and this would be a great way to pay her room and board while creating local references. And just maybe she could sway the Monroes in her favor while she was at it.

Garrett tilted his head. It seemed to her that a tiny light ignited deep within those blue, blue eyes, building into an unnerving glow. "Is that a fact?" he drawled finally.

"Yes. My mother was a florist, and she trained me."

After a moment, Jessa began to wonder what he was staring at. Then Garrett smiled and folded his arms.

"Well," he said, grinning broadly. "Imagine that."

Jessa wasn't sure if that meant the Chatams would welcome her help or not, and he didn't enlighten her. Shaking his head, he turned and left the room, leaving Jessa puzzled in his wake.

Well, at least she and Hunter had a safe place to sleep for the night and it wasn't costing them anything—except a home and a new life.

Jessa slept surprisingly well. Hunter had a bit of trouble settling down in the strange opulence of his room, but eventually he drifted off. Exhausted herself, she'd changed into cotton pajamas and fallen into her own ostentatious bed without even brushing her teeth. Sleep had claimed her almost immediately.

She woke at first light and lay pondering the morning's agenda as the gray dawn yellowed into day. The sound of Hunter's small feet hitting the floor had her sitting up to peer around the brocade hangings at the front of the bed. Hunter darted through her open door, caught the bedpost with one hand and leapt up onto the mattress.

She opened her arms, smiling even as she scolded. "Careful, Hunter. This is expensive antique furniture."

Always quiet, he burrowed into her warm embrace without comment, sighing with contentment. She loved those happy little sounds that he made; they healed the wounds in her heart that his frightened squeaks and shivers inflicted.

He tilted his head back, asking solemnly, "When do we eat?"

She laughed. "As soon as we're dressed, we'll go downstairs and see what we can find." She'd bought groceries at Abby's, but she didn't think the Chatams would appreciate that, and she'd feel foolish offering it.

He ran away. She knew he'd stuff his pajamas into a corner of his suitcase and put on the clothing that she'd laid out the evening before.

"Your toothbrush is in here," she called. She'd prefer that

he didn't use the bath off his bedroom for fear that he'd break something precious.

He returned mere minutes later, allowing her just enough time to change clothes and twist up her hair. After they brushed their teeth, they wandered hand-in-hand across the broad landing and down the grand staircase. It was like something out of a movie, that staircase, all gold marble and dark, glossy wood overhung by a spectacular crystal chandelier anchored to an amazing sky-blue ceiling painted with wafting feathers, ethereal clouds and sparkling sunshine. Hunter could barely walk for gazing upward.

They passed no one as they turned around the newel post and moved down a long hallway that flanked one side of the staircase, only to wind up in a bright sunroom overflowing with wicker and tropical prints. Retracing their steps, they went in the other direction and down the hall that passed by the parlor where their hostesses had gathered the previous night. This time, they found themselves in a darker back hall. The sounds of clanking pots and clinking dishes prompted Jessa to push through a tall swinging door and into the warm, redolent kitchen. Her gaze darted about the amazing room, noting delightful features: a huge fireplace, shuttered windows open to the morning sun, stainless-steel worktables and a massive range.

A large woman with straight hair cropped just below her ears turned from the stove, a spatula in hand. She wore a loose, shapeless dress of brightly flowered fabric under her apron. "The Pagetts, I reckon," she said expressionlessly.

"Yes. He's Hunter, and I'm Jessa."

"Early risers," the woman announced. "I like early risers. I'm Hilda, the cook. Chester, the houseman, is my husband, and my sister Carol's the maid." She waved the spatula at a small, charmingly battered table. "Take a seat. Unless you'd prefer to eat in another room. The misses breakfast next door in the sunroom or take trays upstairs."

"This will suit us fine, if it's no bother," Jessa said, shepherding Hunter toward the table.

"No bother. My job's feeding folks. There's tea, coffee, juice and milk. Help yourselves. How do you take your eggs?"

"We're not particular," Jessa assured the gruff but likable cook.

They were sitting before plates of fluffy scrambled eggs, crisp bacon and plump biscuits before Jessa could taste her coffee. No sooner did she lift a fork, however, than an outside door creaked open and Garrett Willows stepped up into the room.

"Morning, Hilda. What's for breakfast?"

"Eggs and bacon, unless you want a ham steak," came the answer as Hilda shifted a skillet around on the stove.

Garrett clumped across the floor in heavy work boots, heading for the coffee pot. He drew up short when he realized that Jessa and Hunter were seated at the table.

"You're up early."

Jessa nodded and quickly forked egg into her mouth. He poured himself a cup of black coffee and carried it to the table. Pulling out the end chair, he sat and laid one forearm along the edge of the table. Lifting his cup, he sipped then smiled at Hunter.

"Sleep okay?"

Hunter nodded and dropped his gaze to his plate. Garrett turned his blue eyes on Jessa. "He's a quiet one."

"Yes. Yes, he is."

"How about you?"

She felt a bit off-balance, as if he'd just shaken that ladder again. Thankfully, she wasn't about to find herself in his arms this time. Just the memory of that warmed her cheeks. "Uh, am I quiet?"

Garrett grinned. "Actually, I was wondering if you'd slept well, too."

"Oh! I did, yes. Thank you."

He sipped more coffee, eyeing her over the rim of his mug, before drawling, "That makes three of us, then."

Jessa felt her face heat, as he called to the cook, "How about you, Hilda? How did you sleep?"

"Like a two-hundred-and-fifty-pound rock," came the acerbic reply.

Garrett laughed silently into his mug, blue eyes twinkling. Was he making fun of the woman's weight? Even if Hilda was making fun of herself, it seemed crude for him to be so amused.

Jessa tried to ignore him by eating. Unfortunately, she couldn't stop being supremely aware of him. Such fascination made no sense. The man was, if not her enemy, then at least her opponent. What difference did it make how handsome he was or how likable? Who cared if his eyes twinkled when he teased or how tanned and strong his hands looked? She was a fool to even notice such things, but notice she did. She just couldn't seem to help herself, and that puzzled her.

Hilda came and dropped a plate onto the table in front of Garrett. "You didn't say, so you get bacon."

"Bacon suits me to a T," he said, sending a smile up at her. "Is there honey for the biscuits?"

She snorted and waved her spatula. "Of course there's honey for the biscuits. Right over there."

Garrett looked in that direction then literally fluttered his long, inky eyelashes at her, imploring her with a look.

"You'll have to do better than that," she huffed, even as she trundled across the room for the honey pot. She plunked it down in front of him then stayed to talk about wedding cake. "I've been thinking of decorating Ellie's cake with candied violets. That seems like Ellie, doesn't it?"

Garrett nodded, cutting into a trio of over-easy eggs. "I've noticed that she favors purples."

"Well, with those eyes, who wouldn't?" Hilda said.

Jessa had noticed Ellie Monroe's unusual coloring when they'd met. With hair a glossy slate gray and eyes like amethysts, purple would suit Ellie very well.

"We could have candied violets in the ice ring, too," Hilda went on. "Wouldn't that be pretty in a grape punch? And if we had some fresh violets, we could scatter them around the serving tables."

Garrett just grunted and crammed a huge bite of egg-drenched biscuit into his mouth.

Jessa laid down her fork, mind whirling, and carefully inquired, "Where do you intend to get your flowers?"

"From the greenhouse out back," Garrett answered offhandedly.

She gaped at him. "There's a greenhouse?"

He nodded, gobbling bacon. "More than one, actually. We just added the second to the original."

"A real, proper greenhouse?" Jessa pressed.

One corner of his lips hitched up in a lopsided grin. "Why don't you be the judge?" He tucked in more food, chewed perfunctorily and said, "I can show you around when we're done here."

"Really?"

She hadn't meant to sound so eager, especially when she found his company so troubling and he'd just dashed her hopes of supplying any flowers for the weddings. She loved plants, though. They offered beauty without ulterior motive, and peace came as a by-product. In fact, she never felt God's presence more keenly than when surrounded by His leafy creations. Garrett's willingness to afford her the opportunity surprised her, however.

He looked up from his plate, his gaze seeming to indicate that he'd read her thoughts. "I'll be glad to show you around. I like showing off my greenhouse."

"*Your* greenhouse?"

He shrugged. "As the gardener, I have free run of the place."

She nearly dropped her fork. "You're the gardener here?"

"Yep. What'd you think?"

She spread her hands in amazement. "I—I don't know. Abby thought you might be a nephew."

He straightened. "A Chatam nephew? Nope. My sister's married to one, though. Good guy."

"Then you are family."

"Nope." He hunched over his plate again. "My sister is family. I'm just hired help."

Hilda "humphed" but said nothing. Garrett ignored her and, using his remaining biscuit, began mopping up the mess of honey, egg yolk and bacon grease on his plate.

Jessa tried to digest this information, but she couldn't seem to make sense of it all. Family but not family, both Monroes marrying *into* the family, and Garrett Willows turning out to be the gardener. Plus, there was a greenhouse!

Garrett sat back with an "aahh" and patted his flat, firm middle. "Looks like I have violet pots to divide. Thankfully, we have a few weeks left to force some more blooms." He waved a hand at Jessa's plate, saying, "Eat up. We're burning daylight."

Jessa looked down, surprised that her plate remained full while Garrett's had been cleaned. He turned his attention on Hunter, smiling. Hunter froze, glancing to her for guidance, but she didn't know what to signal. She didn't know what to make of Garrett Willows yet. He could be rude or kind, nefarious or an open book, a threat or a blessing. She just didn't know what to think of him. She recalled again how easily he'd caught her when she'd fallen from the ladder, his strong arms supporting her. It had been too long, perhaps forever, since she'd felt so safe with a man, and that, above all, she must not trust. That didn't mean she couldn't take a tour of the greenhouse, though.

In fact, she should tour the greenhouse, she told herself, if only to get a feel for the sort of flowers that the Chatams liked best. Yes, indeed, she told herself, that was wise. It had nothing at all to do with the man next to her with the startling blue eyes.

Nothing whatsoever.

Chapter Three

Jessa gulped down the remainder of her meal, made sure that Hunter thanked Hilda and followed Garrett out the door. She found herself on a narrow, covered walkway that linked a smaller house with the mansion.

"Carriage house," Garrett informed her with a wave of his hand. "All the staff live there."

He was staff, she told herself silently. *And family.* Almost. Sort of. She still didn't know what to make of that.

He led them past a shoulder-high hedge that flanked an expansive patio strewn with wrought-iron furniture and bright potted plants, but the greenhouse some thirty yards away captured Jessa's full attention. She'd seen smaller airplane hangers! Built of glass panels rather than plastic sheeting, the glittering building rose from a lush green lawn artfully transected by wandering walkways of broken paving stone.

"Wow," Jessa said, while standing in the midst of what amounted to a small forest in pots, Hunter's hand in hers. She identified miniature fruit trees and several ornamentals, but the rest were unknown to her.

"The larger trees for outdoor plantings will come after I get the greenhouse built on Charter Street," Garrett told her. "I mean, *if* I get the greenhouse built on Charter Street."

Jessa looked at him, "You're telling me that you want to build a similar nursery at the Monroe place?"

"Actually, I was planning to move this greenhouse there. It belongs to me. Most of it, anyway. I've been planning to open a retail nursery for years, and Magnolia's been helping me by letting me expand the original greenhouse here and load it with stock. She even talked Kent into applying for the combined-use zoning because she thought the Monroe place would be a good site for me."

Jessa winced, deflated. Well, there was the nail in the coffin of her own dreams for the place. "I was planning to open a florist shop in the front room of the house."

He nodded. "So I gathered." Smiling wanly, he added, "Looks like the old adage was right. Great minds do think alike."

Unfortunately, Jessa mused, only one of those "great minds" could claim the property.

"Well, if it's flowers you're interested in," he said, changing the subject, "you should take a look back here."

Gesturing for them to follow, he led her and Hunter through the potted grove and past a well-organized work area. He pushed through a split divider of heavy plastic and into a shocking riot of color.

"Ooooh," Hunter breathed, as intrigued by the display of blossoms as Jessa.

"Are you going to wholesale at some point?" she asked after taking it all in for a minute.

"Hadn't planned on it. Magnolia likes flowers, so this section kind of got out of hand, if you know what I mean."

Hunter pointed at a lush rose bush heavy with glorious orange blossoms. "That's Grandma's flower."

"It is," Jessa told him with an approving smile before explaining to Garrett, "We planted Cinnamon Glow roses on my mother's grave before we moved here."

"I see. Sorry for your loss. Did she pass recently?"

"Five years ago," she replied, oddly touched.

"Almost six for my mom," he said quietly. "Doesn't go away, does it, the feeling of being alone in the world without her?"

"I'm not alone," she replied, squeezing Hunter's small hand, but Garrett was right. Knowing her mother no longer walked this earth left her feeling orphaned.

"What about your dad?" Garrett asked suddenly.

She straightened her shoulders. "I have no idea. He left us and just disappeared."

"That's too bad," Garrett said. "My dad died when I was seven, but I think that might have been better." She jerked her head around and found herself staring straight into eyes the color of the bluest sky imaginable. "I know that he didn't want to leave us because he loved us all so much," Garrett went on, "but that he's well and happy in heaven with the Lord."

"You're right," she told him, gulping and looking away. "That is better. I'd like to see those violets you mentioned."

He seemed to accept the change of subject as gladly as she made it. "Over here." He led her through tables and shelves burdened with too many plants to count. "They're just Common Blue Violets."

"The color is an intense purple, though," Jessa noted, examining dozens of the small, five-petal blossoms, "and they're very healthy."

"I have a few not-so-healthy ones over there," he said, pointing. "I think I can bring those around by the wedding."

"What are you using?"

"I always go organic first."

That started a discussion of organic treatments that carried on far longer than Jessa realized, until Hunter yanked her hand.

"What is it, honey?" She looked down to find him standing with crossed legs and a worried expression on his face.
"Oh."

Garrett, too, got the message. "Hey, the carriage house is
closer. I can run him over there, if you like."

Seeing Hunter's distress, she almost agreed, but then she
realized how close she stood to Garrett and just how long
they had been lost together in conversation, and she mentally berated herself. She knew nothing of this man beyond
his preferred methods of treating various garden pests and
diseases. But a tiny voice in her head argued that they had
more than a love of plants in common: they'd both grown up
fatherless and lost their moms a few years ago, and they were
both Christians.

"He can make it to our rooms. Can't you, sweetie?"

"I'm six, not a baby," the boy said in his little-boy voice.

"Go through the sunroom," Garrett advised. "There's a
men's room in the East Hall, across from the ballroom."

"Thanks," she said, urging Hunter forward. "For the tour,
too."

"No problem," Garrett called after her. "You're both welcome to poke around anytime."

Jessa didn't answer, mostly because she knew that she
should stay away from him. She couldn't risk liking Garrett
Willows any more than she could let herself get too comfortable in a place like Chatam House. East Hall, library,
ballroom, suites, greenhouses that would make commercial
growers weep with joy; Chatam House had it all—including the too-handsome man who had upset all her hopes and
plans.

"Skittish little thing," Garrett muttered, watching Jessa
and Hunter disappear through the divider. The long, verti-

cal strips of heavy plastic flapped and swayed behind them as if to underscore the turmoil that they left in their wake.

He turned back to the violets, heavy of heart. Something was going on with the Pagetts, and it disturbed him plenty. Something about Jessa Lynn Pagett brought out Garrett's protective instincts, and that, he had learned the hard way, was never a good thing. He struggled with that protective part of himself, which often led him to erroneous conclusions and impulsive actions, like the time he'd yanked Chandler Chatam out of his pickup truck and started throwing punches, believing that the man was responsible for Bethany, Garrett's sister, being pregnant and unmarried.

He'd soon found out otherwise, of course, but not until he'd made a real idiot of himself. Thankfully, that episode in stupidity had not created an enemy of the man who was now his brother-in-law and the father of his nephew. Garrett took a moment to thank God for that, smiling to think how happy his sister and her little family were. Obviously, Jessa had not been so blessed.

For one thing, she was divorced. For another, she was clearly overprotective with the boy. Plus, something about her manner signaled that she expected to get the short end of every stick. The boy's quietness and docility bothered Garrett, too. He'd been shocked to hear the kid say that he was six years old. Normal six-year-olds didn't stand silently clasping their moms' hands for the better part of an hour. None that Garret knew, anyway. Still, it wasn't his concern.

Her business ambitions were, though. A florist shop. The Monroe place would be perfect for that. She'd have to be careful not to upset the Historical Society when she put in her shop, but that shouldn't be too tough.

Sighing, he went to work splitting a healthy violet into two shallow pots. While he worked, he pondered the situation with Jessa and the Monroe place.

He could not, in good conscience, fight her on possession of the site. She had a son to house and a business to launch, and unless he missed his guess, she didn't have much funding. Buffalo Creek could certainly use another florist, though, almost as much as a good plant nursery, so she should be okay. He'd tell everyone at the meeting. No point in dragging it out. They were all getting together at some point later today to go over wedding plans and decide the matter of the Monroe place. It could all be settled by nightfall.

Garrett acknowledged a sharp sense of disappointment. The Charter Street site had felt right to him. It felt like home and the future and hope all wrapped up together, but not too long ago a cardboard box would have felt that way to him. He certainly couldn't complain about living and working here at Chatam House. Closing his eyes, he found a silent place within himself and spoke to God.

Guess I jumped the gun in regard to all this, he acknowledged. *Forgive me, Lord.* It wasn't just losing the Monroe place, though. He couldn't help feeling that he was missing out on some sort of opportunity with Jessa and Hunter, too, which was pure nonsense. *At any rate, Your will is always best,* he prayed on. *So that's all I'm asking, for Your will to be done in every aspect of my life. Besides, we both know You've gotten me through much deeper disappointments. You'll get me through this. In the name of Jesus, thanks.*

Feeling a little better, he went back to work. Wouldn't be long, he told himself, before another place came up, one as good for his purposes as the house and lot on Charter Street. Even if the new place wasn't as good, he'd make do and be glad. Meanwhile, Jessa would have her shop and Hunter would have a real home.

Smiling to himself, he recalled Jessa's obvious approval of his greenhouse and plants. He saw her in his mind's eye, her big dark eyes surveying his little domain with pleasure. The image of her face had not been far from his mind since he'd first laid eyes on it.

He wondered what she was going to do with her day. Maybe he should look in on her and Hunter later. Then again, maybe he should mind his own business.

"Ms. Pagett," Magnolia said, pausing on the stairway beside Hypatia to acknowledge the young woman and her son.

"Oh, call me Jessa, ma'am."

"Very well. We'll all be on a first-name basis, then. Much easier that way."

Hypatia bent forward slightly and spoke to the boy. "How are you this morning, Hunter?"

"Fine," he answered softly. His mother gave his hand a waggle, and he added, "Thank you."

Hypatia smiled. "My, you are a well-mannered young man."

"Thank you," he and his mother said at the same time.

Magnolia opened her mouth to ask how they'd slept, but the sound of a buzz saw had her grimacing instead. Tossing a resigned glance upward, she offered Jessa a wan smile. The screech of the buzz saw ceased, leaving abrupt silence. Magnolia offered her apologies.

"It never lasts very long. Mr. Bowen is a most considerate fellow."

Jessa nodded as she slipped past the two older women, tugging her son behind her. "No problem. Excuse us, please. We have books waiting."

"Did you find the library, then?" Magnolia asked, pointing to the door below, across the foyer from the front parlor.

"Not yet. I meant our lesson books, ma'am," Jessa clarified, hurrying Hunter around the curve in the stairs.

Magnolia tilted her head at that, but Hypatia just sighed and resumed her descent. Magnolia fell in beside her sister, trying not to smile at Hypatia's exasperation.

"What happened to hand saws?" she asked. "I'm sure they were more accurate."

The things that upset the usually unflappable Hypatia always amused Magnolia. Every flower, tree, shrub and blade of grass on the place could die overnight, and Hypatia wouldn't blink an eye, but forget one little rule of etiquette or upset her routine, and she groused. Politely, of course. True to form, Hypatia waited until they were safely in the sunroom and out of earshot of anyone who might be offended before she complained.

"Really. Guests while the house is undergoing construction! Not to mention planning two weddings. How are we to be proper hostesses with that *racket* going on and our focus consumed with getting Ellie and Asher married?"

"Most of the time, we don't even know Mr. Bowen is around," Magnolia pointed out.

"Nevertheless, I wish he'd get on with it," Hypatia grumbled.

"You're the one who told the Historical Society that we would use materials only from the period when the house was built."

Hypatia made a face. "I'm not the one who invited the Pagetts to stay without consulting another soul, however."

"What could I do?" Magnolia asked. "The Pagetts were obviously in dire straits."

"And you didn't want them moving into the Monroe house," Hypatia surmised flatly.

"Much more difficult to evict them than host them," Magnolia conceded.

"And are you so confident that Garrett will win the day?" Hypatia asked.

Magnolia chose not to answer that. "I'm confident that the hand of God is at work here."

Hypatia arched an eyebrow, but Magnolia took her time settling onto the chaise longue of her choice. Spreading her dark plaid skirts around her, she lightly asked, "Do you know why Jessa Lynn Pagett wants to lease the Monroe place?"

"It's a lovely house in which to raise a child, I imagine."

"It's also a great site for a florist shop," Magnolia said. "Garrett told me last night that she's a florist, and she herself said she was opening a shop there."

Hypatia let that sink in. "A florist, is she? Well, well."

"Exactly," Magnolia said with a satisfied lift of her chin. "A florist and a gardener."

Hypatia tapped the cleft in her chin with one gleaming fingertip. "It's something to think about, I must say. We've seen matches made of less."

Magnolia crossed her ankles and folded her hands. "Indeed. Just look at Ellie and Asher."

"Or Chandler and Bethany."

"Or Reeves and Anna! Not to mention…" They both laughed, eyes twinkling as they thought of Odelia and Kent coming together again after a half century apart. "So you agree with me that it's a matter for prayer."

"Definitely," Hypatia said.

They smiled in perfect accord. Then Hypatia touched the pearls at her throat.

"About the meeting this afternoon," she said. "I really can't abide the idea of another buffet." She was still miffed that Ellie and Asher had stood firm on a buffet for their wedding reception. Worse, Hilda agreed with them! Personally, it seemed the only sensible solution to Magnolia at this late juncture, but Hypatia would never be entirely happy about the matter. "Surely, we can hire a decent number of wait staff for the June wedding. Don't you agree?"

Magnolia rolled her eyes. Suggest that to Odelia, and she'd be out scouring the DFW Metroplex for waiters of identical height, weight, complexion and hair color—and rainbow-hued tuxedoes to outfit them. Magnolia chuckled, wondering just how pleased Hypatia would be then.

"At least," she said hopefully, "God has provided us with a genuine florist."

"Ah, yes," Hypatia agreed, nodding. "There is that."

And, Magnolia hoped, much more.

"Very good," Jessa praised, watching Hunter practice the last of his letters in his copybook.

"Done now, Mommy?" he asked hopefully.

They'd taken several breaks throughout the day. He'd watched his favorite program on TV and played with the tiny cars that were his personal delight. The remainder of his few toys were stuffed in a box stacked with several others in Abby's tiny living room. Jessa wondered if she ought to move the boxes here. Chatam House certainly had more space for such things.

She shook her head. Chances were that she and Hunter would be out of here today or tomorrow. Where exactly they'd go, she didn't know, but surely she could afford a cheap motel for a couple days until they could return to Abby's. Then what? A knock at the sitting-room door derailed that unhappy speculation.

"Come in."

A fortyish woman with long, lank, dark blond hair opened the door and peeked into the room. "I'm Carol, the house-maid."

"Oh, yes. Your sister mentioned you earlier."

Carol slipped fully into the room. Dressed in polyester pants and a cotton blouse, she did not quite meet Jessa's image of a maid, but then the cook had worn a flowered muumuu under her apron that morning. "The misses would like you to come down to the library now, if it's convenient. Miss Ellie and Mr. Asher have arrived."

Jessa's heart leapt into her throat. So the moment had come. It was sooner than she'd expected, not even 3:00 p.m. She patted Hunter's hand comfortingly and rose from the floor in front of the coffee table where they had conducted their lessons. "We'll be right down."

"I'll stay with the boy," Carol volunteered, "if you like."

Jessa glanced at Hunter, who gave his head the tiniest of nods. "Thank you, Carol. I'll try not to be long."

"Oh, don't rush on my account," Carol said, moving across the room to seat herself on the couch. "I like kids. Would a snack be okay? Fruit and maybe a cookie or two? Nothing to ruin the young man's dinner." Hunter perked up noticeably.

"That would be fine," Jessa said with a smile, moving toward the door.

Hunter's eyes twinkled at Jessa as she backed from the room. She knew that in many ways her little boy was not as mature as others of his age, but he possessed a quiet sense of humor rivaling that of any adult.

Taking down her hair as she traversed the landing, Jessa combed through it with her fingers and twisted it up again, expertly fixing the clip in place. She hadn't reached the curve in the broad staircase before silky strands drifted down to waft about her face. She blew one out of her eyes with a puff of air from between her lips and wondered if she should have changed her cheap canvas tennis shoes for dressier flats. Then again, if winning the day depended upon her attire, she'd be lost before she'd begun.

The door to which Magnolia had pointed earlier now stood open, and muted voices filtered through it, along with the soft rumble of laughter. Her heart pounding, Jessa paused on the stairs to gather her courage.

Now would be the time, Lord, she found herself praying. *If ever You're going to answer my prayers, now would be the time. For my son's sake, and in the name of Your Son, please.*

Inhaling deeply, she moved on down to the foyer and crossed over to the library door. She'd seen public libraries with less to offer. Bookshelves lined every wall, and a long, interesting table, surrounded by chairs, occupied the center of the densely carpeted floor, with a number of people standing and sitting around it. Hilda dropped into a chair, obviously having just placed an ornate silver tea service on the table. Heads turned in Jessa's direction, but before she could speak, she felt a presence at her back.

"Hello, everyone," Garrett called out cheerfully.

A light touch near her waist literally propelled her into the room. Kent Monroe came to his feet, Odelia clinging to his hand. For a moment, Jessa couldn't tear her eyes from the woman, who wore an aqua turban, chandelier earrings hung with multicolored stones, and a shocking pink caftan trimmed with rainbow fringe.

"We're meeting early today," Garrett said to no one in particular.

A slender man in an expensive suit turned from a private conversation with Ellie Monroe and smiled. A rosy gray painted the temples of his chestnut hair and called attention to his glittering amber eyes. If they were not enough to mark him as a Chatam, the cleft chin certainly was.

"It's an early release day at the school," he said. He came around the end of the table, his hand outstretched. "Ms. Pagett, I presume. I'm Asher Chatam."

Jessa shook his hand, and said, "Nice to meet you."

Ellie came to offer an apologetic hug. "Jessa, I'm so sorry about what's happened. I had no idea Grandpa had spoken to Garrett about the house."

"We'll sort it out, sweetheart," Asher told Ellie, sliding

his arm around her to cup his hand over her shoulder. She wrapped her arm around his waist, smiling up at him as if he'd hung the moon.

Jessa felt a stab of envy. She'd seen that look before. In her wedding photos. Unfortunately it hadn't lasted a month.

At Hypatia's urging, they all gathered around the table, the Chatam triplets, Kent and Ellie Monroe, Asher, the cook Hilda, Garrett and Jessa. After pulling out a chair for Jessa, Garrett managed to find himself a seat opposite her next to Magnolia. Asher took the spot at the head of the table, Ellie on his right, while Kent remained at the foot with Odelia next to him.

Hypatia began passing out tea, starting with Jessa.

"Thank you," she began, "but—"

Garrett cleared his throat loudly then declared, "This is nice. One benefit of meeting early. A cup of tea is always nice. *Especially* around here."

Jessa blinked. Had he just sent her a message? She caught the expectant expression on Hypatia Chatam's face, took the hint and reached for the teacup. Eyeing the three sugar cubes on the accompanying saucer, Jessa carefully amended her comment.

"I—I really don't need sugar."

Smiling, Hypatia quickly switched saucers, confiding, "I take my own tea black, but nearly everyone else sweetens theirs."

"Some of us more than others," Kent acknowledged, plunking four of the cubes into his own cup and then reaching for a small plate of finger sandwiches.

Jessa carefully tasted the tea and found it surprisingly pleasant. Hypatia's demeanor told her that she'd just passed a kind of test. Jessa glanced at Garrett with gratitude in her eyes. He acknowledged it with a slight dip of his head, and she quickly looked away again.

Oh, it would not do to *like* him. Gratitude was one thing, but liking was something else altogether, the first step on a dangerous path that could only lead to heartbreak. He was her adversary, not her friend. If only he weren't so breathtakingly handsome....

Chapter Four

"So," Asher Chatam said, effortlessly taking command of the meeting, "here's what I gather so far. Ellie spoke with Jessa at the school about nine-thirty yesterday morning, Wednesday. They made an agreement for Jessa to lease the house on Charter Street and Ellie received a check, which she has not deposited."

"Yes," Ellie said.

"Ellie then told Jessa that she could go ahead and move into the house." He looked pointedly to Ellie, adding, "Even though I hadn't yet had a chance to draw up papers." Ellie gave a little shrug, smiling wanly. Clearly, Jessa noted, she was not troubled by his thinly veiled scold.

"At about the same time as Ellie was talking to Jessa," Asher went on, "Kent spoke to Garrett here at Chatam House about a lease/purchase agreement. They agreed on a monthly consideration, and funds were deposited with Kent to seal the deal."

"Uh, no," Garrett interrupted. "That's not correct. No money changed hands on our end."

Kent cleared his throat, and Magnolia sighed. "Actually," she muttered, "money did change hands, so to speak."

"She had the money transferred into my bank account," Kent clarified.

Garrett closed his eyes and shook his head. "And you were going to tell me this when?"

"When you needed to know," Magnolia answered primly.

He clamped his jaw, looking away. An uncomfortable silence ensued, broken moments later by Asher. "Well," he said, "there you have it. One property. Two legally identical transactions."

"Quite the coincidence," Jessa mumbled.

"Oh, my dear," Hypatia said with a chuckle that proved the acuity of her hearing, "we don't believe in coincidences around here, not for God's children."

"Indeed, not," Magnolia commented.

"A coincidence is just God at work," Odelia tittered.

"That's good," Asher said, "because we're going to need some divine guidance to resolve this. Unless...." He looked from Garrett, who appeared to be brooding, to Jessa who, admittedly, was doing a bit of the same. *Unless what?* she wondered, but before she could ask for clarification, Magnolia spoke up again.

"I propose that we put this issue aside until after Ellie and Asher's wedding." Jessa bit her lip in dismay, but Magnolia hurried on. "Of course, Jessa and Hunter will remain here with us as our guests in the meantime."

"But the wedding's a month away, isn't it?" Jessa spoke up quickly. "We couldn't impose that long."

"It's no imposition," Magnolia insisted, sitting forward. "More like a blessing." She glanced around the table, adding pointedly, "Jessa just happens to be a florist."

"That's true," Ellie chimed in, "and I admit that when she told me about wanting to open her own shop at the house on Charter Street, I immediately thought about asking her to help out with the wedding." She looked to Jessa, saying, "I meant to let you get settled first."

"Well, I'm happy to be of assistance, of course," Jessa said, brightening, "especially if it will help cover our room and board here."

"Now, now," Hypatia interrupted. "None of that. Our guests do not worry about room and board. We will pay you for your help, of course."

"Sounds like a plan to me," Asher commented, sitting back in his chair.

"Me, too!" Ellie declared.

Jessa beamed. This could all work out in her favor, after all. She already had most of the material she would need, other than the flowers, and she could find many of those in the greenhouse. More importantly, if she did a good job for them, Ellie and Asher just might start to argue on her behalf in regard to the Monroe place. Staying here wasn't the same as Hunter and her having their own home, of course, but it wasn't exactly slumming, either, and they wouldn't have to impose on Abby, at least not for a good while.

"Now that that's settled," Hilda said, "could we finalize the menu? This May wedding isn't exactly a small family affair. Not that there's any such thing with the Chatams."

Conversation shifted to food and then to the guest list, which was considerable. Finally, Hilda rose to depart, saying that she had to start dinner.

"And I have another meeting," Asher said apologetically, already on his feet.

"Thanks for working around my schedule," Ellie told him, turning her face up to receive his kiss.

"I'm happy to work around your schedule, sweetheart," he told her.

They murmured between themselves for several seconds before he left the room. Jessa tried not to watch, only to have her gaze land on Garrett. He seemed troubled, caught in his own thoughts, until Asher left, at which point he roused himself and turned to Ellie.

"About the violets…"

"I think they'll be perfect on the cake," she gushed. "Don't you?"

"Those are candied violets," Garrett pointed out. "That's not my department, but I have several dozen potted violets that we can use for decoration. I'm just not sure they'll be enough to strike a real theme, you know?"

"I think you're right," Jessa interjected quickly. "I suggest going with mixed bouquets with as many purples as we can find."

Ellie clapped her hands. "Excellent. Why don't you meet with Garrett and figure out what we can use, then maybe put together something I can look at?"

"I've already seen the greenhouse, so I can go ahead and draw up some designs," Jessa told her.

"What a blessing you are!" Ellie exclaimed, coming around the table to hug her again. "And after all the mix-up, too! Don't you worry, though, it'll all work out. Right, Garrett?"

"Right." He nodded, smiling wanly. "Wedding, property issues, all of it."

Beaming, Ellie danced away, her hopes and dreams secure. Jessa wished that she could be so sure about her own life, but she had never been among the blessed, not like these people.

No matter. Things had been worse, much worse. Maybe her life wasn't what she'd hoped it would be at this moment, but it was a far cry from what it had been, and her son would never, never again, live with fear. She would uphold that vow, whatever it took.

Right now, that would have to be enough.

* * *

As Jessa excused herself and hurried from the room, Garrett looked around for Magnolia. Knowing that she would be eager to avoid him, he didn't bother looking in her chair. He found her speaking to Odelia and Kent. She skirted the balding, portly old gent, making a beeline for Ellie.

Garrett trailed her, arriving in time to hear Ellie say, "I think you're right. I'm sure she'll be a great help. Frankly, I'm a little concerned about the boy, though."

"What about the boy?" Garrett couldn't help asking.

"Well, Jessa's homeschooling," Ellie said, "and while I'm not against homeschooling on principle, I do wonder if Hunter is being socialized enough. He seems unusually timid and quiet."

Given Ellie's occupation as a kindergarten teacher, Garrett wasn't surprised at her conclusion. He'd made a similar judgment himself earlier, but something compelled him to defend the boy.

"That might not have anything to do with his schooling. He could just be naturally shy."

"That's true," Ellie conceded, "but he would still need large-group experience to help him overcome his natural tendency to fade into the background."

"Couldn't he get that, say, at church?" Garrett pressed.

"Possibly."

"He's certainly well-mannered," Magnolia observed, "but he does stick close to his mother. You don't suppose he was bullied in the past, do you? I've heard of that happening to quiet children."

Bullied, Garrett thought, his heart sinking, *or, more likely, abused.* He fervently hoped that was not the case, but he'd already recognized the signs. Maybe he'd find out the truth while he and Jessa worked on the flowers for the wedding.

He certainly didn't mind the idea of working with her.

She seemed to have a good eye and even if her skills turned out to be only mediocre, they would be better than his or Magnolia's when it came to bouquets and such. Besides, he didn't exactly find her repulsive. Prickly, yes, but somehow that only added to her appeal. That didn't really explain why he'd kept his mouth shut about backing out of his deal with Kent, though.

He'd intended to do it, and Asher had clearly expected it of him or Jessa. In his defense, Garrett had been momentarily blindsided by Magnolia's admission concerning the money. When they'd talked, Kent had detailed the kind of investment that would be expected in order to finalize the deal, but he hadn't asked for the money then. Garrett had assumed that it would be expected at the signing of the papers. He'd never dreamed that Magnolia would take it upon herself to pay the funds herself. That reminded him why he was standing there.

Tugging at her sleeve, he cleared his throat. "I need a word with you, please."

Ellie split an amused look between them. "I promised to spend a few minutes with Grandpa," she said, pirouetting off in Kent's direction. "You'd think we were never going to see each other again after I move into Asher's house."

"Now, Garrett," Magnolia began immediately.

"It was very generous of you to give Kent cash out of your own account, but you know I can't accept your money," Garrett said.

"I only wanted—"

"I *have* money," he went on firmly, "and I would have paid Kent what he needed when we signed the papers."

"But I have so much more than—"

"It goes back into your account, Magnolia. Every penny."

"Why do you have to be so stubborn?" she grumbled.

Grinning, he bent and smacked a kiss on her leathery cheek. "Why do *you?*"

She folded her arms, fighting a smile. Garrett left her there, wondering yet again why he hadn't just ended the whole debacle earlier by dropping his claim to the Charter Street site. As he hurried back to his duties, Garrett admitted the truth. He didn't drop his claim because then Jessa Lynn Pagett and her too-quiet son would leave Chatam House for good. Before he knew them better. Before he knew *her* better. Before he knew the truth about them.

Before he knew why he couldn't stop thinking about her or looking forward to their next encounter.

Garrett stayed busy that evening. He ignored Magnolia's summons to the dinner table, knowing that if he let her turn him up sweet now, she'd harass him about accepting her money. Instead, he made a little space in the greenhouse by moving some of the topiaries outside to the patio, something he should have done a week or so earlier. After that, he gathered up all of the containers scattered around the building. After a late supper in the kitchen, he stopped by the family parlor in hopes of arranging to meet with Jessa and Magnolia the next day.

Jessa was nowhere to be seen, however. She and Hunter had declined to join the family for dinner, too. Garrett told himself that they were not avoiding him, just still settling in, but then Hilda reported the next morning that not only had they elected to take dinner in their suite the night before, but also breakfast. Garrett nursed a secret emotional bruise while demolishing a bowl of Hilda's grits with stewed pears, then headed out to the greenhouse to seek out every purple flower he could find and some ferns he'd had in mind.

The instant he stepped through the door, he knew someone was there. Glancing around, he eased through the front space and into the next, slipping through the heavy plastic curtain. Surprised at whom he found there among the flowers, he took a moment to make certain that his voice remained calm and level.

"Hello."

The boy whirled away from the rose bush to face Garrett, tension in every line of the small body inside his oversize clothes. "I didn't touch it," he said.

"Okay." Hunter's hands trembled at his sides, so Garrett casually bent to shift a container and clear the pathway a bit. "It won't hurt if you touch it, though. Just be careful you don't get scratched by a thorn. That variety has some big ones."

"It does?"

He heard the curiosity in the boy's voice and smiled to himself. "Yeah, it does. Check it out." Moving closer, Garrett carefully parted the heavy, rust-colored blossoms. "See? That's a nasty thorn right there."

The boy peered at the sharp, green protuberance as if expecting it to jump out and bite him. Then he looked at Garrett with puzzlement in his dark eyes.

"It's a protective mechanism," Garrett explained, "to keep animals like cows from eating the bushes down to the ground. If that had happened, roses would have vanished long before we were able to propagate them. Grow them for ourselves, I mean. And wouldn't that be a shame? A world without roses."

"Mommy likes roses."

Garrett smiled. "Me, too. Thorns and all. But we have to know that sometimes beautiful things are also dangerous."

"Like what?"

"Well, think of an eagle. Beautiful, right?" Hunter gave a tiny nod. "Or a bear." This time he got a hint of a smile. "Or even a snake." Hunter pulled his lips down and back in an expression of distaste. Garrett laughed. "Hey, I've seen some really beautiful snakeskin boots." A husky chuckle escaped the boy. "You want to see something else?" Garrett asked, suddenly inspired.

Hunter nodded and followed as Garrett gestured and moved deeper into the tables and rows of flowers.

"I only have one, and it's not all that pretty, in my opinion, but it is fascinating." He came to the table with the terrarium. "This is a Venus Fly Trap. It never has more than seven leaves. One day it will have a very tall flower, but not just yet. Guess what I feed it?" Hunter's brow furrowed. "All plants eat," Garrett explained. "They eat by absorbing nutrients from the soil, air and light, but this plant eats *insects*."

"Huh?"

"That's right. I feed it bugs that I pick off the plants outside. Watch." Garrett carefully picked a leaf from an azalea, rolled a section of it into a tight ball and stuck it on the end of a piece of wire. "Pretend this is a bug." He touched the leaf ball to the inside of one of the spiny leaves, which immediately folded over it. Hunter gasped. Garrett wiggled the wire until the leaf ball came off the end. The trap slowly closed around the azalea leaf. "Since that's not a bug, it'll spit it out in a few hours, but we'll get some real bugs and feed the other leaves."

Hunter beamed. "Cool."

"It is kind of cool, isn't it?" Garrett said. "Now, want to tell me why you're here?"

Hunter shrugged. "Mommy's working in her room. She said I could do lessons or play. I didn't want to do lessons."

Garrett grinned. "Not much room to play in here."

The boy pulled a pair of diecast cars from his pockets and looked up at him.

"Okay," Garrett said, moving toward the potting bench. "I have some stuff to do over here. You can come along if you want."

As Garrett thought he might, the boy followed. He settled down at the end of the bench and began to run his cars around the rim of an empty plastic pot. Smiling, Garrett went about his business. At least one of the Pagetts wasn't avoiding him.

Garrett worked in silence for a few minutes, then felt compelled to engage the boy again, but how did he start a conversation with a six-year-old? After thinking a moment, he asked, "What's your full name?"

Several long seconds of silence later, Garrett glanced at the boy and found himself being regarded with a solemn expression. Finally, the boy whispered, "I'm not s'posed to tell."

A shock ran through Garrett, but he maintained a calm expression, saying, "Yeah? I'm not supposed to know your middle name? Mine's Jackson. My mom's last name was Jackson before she married my dad, so it was her way of naming me after my grandfather."

"I'm named after my grandfather, too," Hunter immediately reported. "No," he amended, his brow furrowing. "Mommy's grandfather."

"Your great-grandfather, then. And what was his name?"

"Lynn."

Garrett smiled. "So you're named after your mom *and* your great-grandfather. That's neat."

"My mom, her mom and her grandfather," Hunter corrected.

"Oh? Your mother's mother was named Lynn, too?"

The boy shook his head. "Pagett."

"Ah." So the name that Hunter wasn't supposed to tell was his last name, Pagett clearly being Jessa's maiden name or her mother's maiden name. Garrett felt cold in the pit of his belly. They were hiding. But from whom?

"Hunter Lynn Pagett is a good name," Garrett said lightly, betraying none of his suspicions.

Smiling, Hunter went back to his play. Garrett told himself that he could be mistaken. But he wasn't. Somehow, he knew that he was not mistaken in his assumption that this mother and son were in hiding.

The theory proved true when Jessa appeared, breathless and wild-eyed, her hair streaming from the clip on the back of her head. She clutched a sketchpad in one hand, the other fisted around a pencil.

"Hunter is—"

The boy stood up, moving quickly to her. For a moment, she seemed about to collapse in her relief. Instead, she quickly put herself between Garrett and the boy.

"I'm sorry!" she exclaimed, grasping that pencil like a spear. "This is my fault." She turned her head, hissing at the boy, "What were you thinking?"

"To play," he whispered back.

"This is not a place to play!"

"It's fine," Garrett told her, leaning back against the side of the potting table. "I told you that you were welcome anytime, and I meant it."

"It won't happen again," she insisted.

"Really. It's okay. He knows he can't run around in here. Right?" Hunter nodded solemnly. "So, if he wants to play in here, no problem."

"You say that now," Jessa began.

"If I change my mind, I'll let you know," Garrett interrupted pointedly, "but he's not exactly the rambunctious type, is he?" She clamped her lips into a flat line. Garrett changed the subject, nodding toward the sketchpad. "Do you have something there you want to show me?"

She lifted it to her chest, holding it close for a moment, then she walked to the bench, laid the sketchpad atop it and flipped open the cover. Garrett glanced at the top drawing, lightly colored with pencil, and then at her before picking up the pad and turning the page.

"These are fantastic. Ellie will be thrilled."

Jessa beamed. "You think?"

"I've never seen drawings like these."

"I have photos," she said quickly, "but not with me, and I like to draw, so I thought I'd do it this way. The actual designs wouldn't be exact, of course, but this gives you the idea."

"We're going to need ribbon," he muttered, looking at the designs.

"No problem. I know where to get everything. I have accounts, established by my mother, with all the wholesalers in Dallas."

Pleased, Garrett quipped, "Well, aren't you a little ray of sunshine." She laughed, and the sound flowed over his skin like water on a parched throat. "I don't have any of these tiny mums or purple roses, but there's hyacinth and hollyhock over here, and I have some really delicate ferns you should see."

He led her to a small space filled with potted ferns and lifted one from the floor. Jessa stepped up to finger the delicate, pale gray-green velvet of the frond. "It's beautiful and the stems are stiff enough to work well. If Ellie's okay with it, I certainly am."

"Let me show you something that might work for Odelia's wedding," he suggested quickly, setting aside the first fern. "She's a little more flamboyant than Ellie."

"A little?"

He had to grin. "Okay, a lot. But she's as sweet as she is odd."

"You're genuinely fond of them, aren't you?" Jessa said, sounding bemused.

"The Chatam sisters? I adore them," Garrett admitted unabashedly.

She stared at him for several seconds before shaking her

head. "I suppose I should thank you for yesterday. The tea, I mean."

He shrugged. "The Chatams are serious about their tea, and I'm not sure they quite trust anyone who doesn't enjoy it. I couldn't stand hot tea when I first came here, frankly, but I soon learned to appreciate an afternoon cup."

"I see. Basically, then, you started drinking it so they'd trust you?"

"No," he said. "I started drinking it because I didn't want to hurt their feelings. I signaled you to drink it so they'd trust *you.*"

"Why would you do that?"

He tilted his head in surprise. "Why not? You seem trust-worthy to me. You are, aren't you?"

"Of course, I am." She lifted her chin and changed the subject yet again. "You wanted to show me another fern we could use for the second wedding?"

He folded his arms, refusing to be budged this time. "You should know something else about the Chatams."

"Oh?" Her gaze stubbornly evaded his, but he plowed ahead.

"You'll offend them if you keep refusing to join them for dinner."

Her dainty jaw firmed, lips pressing together in a stern line. "We aren't the kind to take advantage or impose."

"Look, I'm not suggesting that you take advantage of anyone. I just don't see why you have to hurt their feelings."

Finally, she looked at him. "How am I hurting their feelings?"

"By refusing their hospitality. They believe it's their Christian duty to offer hospitality to everyone they bump into on the street. They *pride* themselves on their hospitality. And, I assure you, it's offered without any expectation other than acceptance."

Jessa might have looked a tad embarrassed, but she looked away too quickly for him to be sure. "I'll keep that in mind."

Sighing inwardly, he let it go. He didn't know why he even bothered. She might look like an adorable doll, but Jessa Lynn Pagett could be hard as nails.

"The other ferns are right over here," he told her.

"Ah." She made a comment about the color, and soon they were involved in an animated conversation about the different possibilities—until something crashed. Garrett knew the sound well. A terracotta pot had fallen and shattered, a common occurrence around any greenhouse. The natural conclusion was that Hunter had bumped into something, but before Garrett could comment on that fact, Jessa took off in a panic. Garrett followed at a slightly more sedate pace, sure that the boy would have cried out if he'd been hurt. He arrived on the scene to find the pair of them staring down at a pile of red-orange shards with twin expressions of horror.

Jessa whirled, exclaiming, "It was an accident."

"Of course, it was an accident," Garrett replied calmly, reaching for a broom and dustpan.

"I'm to blame," Jessa insisted, placing herself between him and the boy once again, as if expecting Garrett to go after the child with the broomstick. The idea sickened him. He didn't like being presumed a brute, but he liked even less the idea that someone had brutalized these two. And someone definitely had.

Pushing aside the irritation, he made himself speak in a light, even tone. "No one's to blame. Accidents happen."

Hunter leaned to the side, peering out from around his mother. "I didn't mean to," he whispered.

"I know," Garrett said, moving around Jessa to sweep up the mess. "You didn't get cut, did you?" Hunter shook his head. "Good."

Garrett carried the laden dustpan to the workbench and

pulled out a box. "I break pots all the time," he told the boy, dumping the shards into the box. "This is where I keep the broken pieces, then I use them later in the bottoms of other pots so the soil doesn't clog the drainage holes." He set aside the dustpan and turned to face Hunter, who now stood next to his mother. "Be a little more careful next time, okay, buddy?"

"Yes, sir."

Garrett smiled, reached out and ruffled the boy's hair, saying, "You're a good kid, you know that?"

Hunter looked stunned, shocked, and then his dark eyes began to gleam. The next thing Garrett knew, Jessa had bodily turned the boy and rushed him out of there. It happened so fast that Garrett stood there blinking at the empty spot where they had been. After a moment, Garrett smoothed a hand over his forehead and sighed.

What had happened to those two?

And what, if anything, was he supposed to do about it?

Chapter Five

"There, now," Magnolia said, beaming at Jessa and Hunter as they pulled their chairs up to the table. "Very cozy."

Jessa glanced around the cavernous room, with its dark woods, ornate plaster fireplace, chandelier and old-fashioned floral wallpaper, and thought it was anything but cozy. They could probably seat eighteen for dinner at the massive table without crowding anyone. The table looked almost bare with the current eight around it. Make that nine.

Garrett slipped through the door, joining the three Chatam sisters, Kent and Ellie Monroe, Asher Chatam, and Jessa and Hunter. He had obviously changed clothes and shaved since they'd met in the greenhouse. It seemed unfair that he could look so good in a simple black T-shirt, jeans and round-toed boots. She felt worn in her usual old jeans and simple blouse, but she simply didn't have enough wardrobe to change for dinner every evening. Looking as uncomfortable as she felt, Garrett pulled out a chair for Magnolia, then seated himself between her and Asher, who had dressed down for the event, like Ellie, in running clothes. Jessa had the impression that the two actually intended to go out for a run at some point after the meal.

From the head of the table, Hypatia asked everyone to

join hands for prayer, which she asked Asher to deliver. He did so, thanking God for all present, the food and the hands that prepared it, as well as a number of other blessings. Jessa squeezed Hunter's hand to let him know that he was one of her blessings. The "amens" were said, and she opened her eyes, only to find herself looking directly into a pair of bright blue ones. Garrett. Unaccountably flustered, she gave her heavy linen napkin more attention than it merited then bent to hear Hunter whisper that he had too many forks.

"One is for your salad, honey," she whispered back, watching a heavy crystal bowl being passed around the table. He looked confused but said nothing else.

The salad turned out to be loaded with mandarin oranges and apple chunks, two of Hunter's favorite foods. Steaming slices of fresh bread won his instant approval, too, especially when he was allowed to have butter. He hardly knew what to do with the salmon croquette, but the macaroni and cheese disappeared almost instantly, and she only had to remind him to eat his broccoli a couple times. His dark eyes grew wider with every new addition to the meal carried to the table by the houseman, Chester, Hilda's balding husband, and Jessa felt a pang of guilt.

This was simply dinner to these people, but it was a feast to her son. The two of them normally would have made do with the macaroni and cheese plus a green veggie, but they had eaten quite well since coming to Chatam House. She reminded herself that a growing boy needed more food than his cautious-with-a-penny mother and silently promised that she would find a way to provide him with more bountiful meals when they left here.

She could tell that he was full to bursting by the time dessert came, but the pears baked with a crunchy topping proved too much for him to resist, especially as it was accompanied by ice cream. She let him eat what he could manage, wished she could refrigerate the rest for later and tried to pay attention to the conversation around the dinner table, which naturally focused mainly on the upcoming weddings.

Hypatia expressed discontent with the buffet planned for Ellie and Asher's wedding, arguing instead for a meal "properly served at table."

Ellie explored other alternatives. "Maybe family style. Like this."

Hypatia nearly swallowed her ice cream spoon. Jessa privately mused that if this was what passed for a family-style dinner at Chatam House, she'd be too terrified to eat a "properly served" meal. Hypatia agreed to the buffet without further argument.

"Well, now that that's settled, I can concentrate on flowers and a gown," Ellie said happily.

"Speaking of flowers," Garrett put in, casting a glance in Jessa's direction, "you should see Jessa's designs."

Ellie gasped with delight. "You have designs already?"

"They're just a starting point," Jessa said.

"I think they're magnificent," Garrett stated flatly. "They're imaginative, striking, gorgeous. I think they're you, Ellie. I think she read you and put you in those designs. You'll see."

Ellie literally clapped her hands. "When? When can I see?"

"A-anytime," Jessa told her, fighting down the surge of delight that she'd felt at Garrett's praise.

"Right now," Ellie proclaimed, shoving back her chair. She grabbed Asher's arm saying, "This won't take long. We need to let our dinner settle before we hit the track, anyway."

"No problem," he replied indulgently. "We have all evening. The track's lighted."

Ellie kissed him quickly then said to Ellie, "I'll meet you in the library!"

"Ooh, me, too!" Odelia twittered, hastily getting to her feet.

Kent, who had managed to rise only halfway before both women disappeared, glanced around the table at the others. Magnolia and Hypatia were both calmly folding their dinner napkins, but they took the hint and quickly got up. Jessa followed suit.

"The boy's welcome to stay with us while you ladies rhapsodize over flowers," Kent told Jessa. "I promise not to break out the port and cigars. Actually, we don't have any port or cigars." He laughed.

"Which is understandable since we don't drink or smoke," Asher commented with a chuckle.

Jessa looked to Hunter, who seemed perfectly content where he was. "I won't be long."

She hurried to slip past the older ladies, saying, "I'll just run up and get my sketchpad."

Behind them, Asher chuckled as Kent said, "I believe I'll have another pear."

Jessa sprinted up the stairs. Grabbing the sketchpad from the desk, she ran back down again, pausing at the foot of the stairs to catch her breath before swinging around the newel post. Garrett lounged in the library doorway as if he'd been waiting for hours.

"You don't mind if I join you, do you?" he asked, straightening and stepping back.

His blue gaze holding hers, he lifted an arm to indicate that she should precede him, which she did, her heart pounding a little harder than it had a moment before. How did he do that to her with just a look? She tried to tell herself that it was because he'd praised her work earlier, but she knew better. Even that morning when she'd feared that he would attempt to discipline her son, she'd been aware that her quickened pulse had as much to do with the man himself and her attraction to him as her fears. She wasn't the only one charmed by him, either. When Hunter had looked at him with worshipful eyes, she'd panicked and whisked him out of the greenhouse.

She felt a little foolish now. Garrett would never be more than a temporary part of their lives. He didn't have the power to disappoint or wound her son, and she would make sure that he never gained it because even if he wasn't the strike-first-explain-later sort, that didn't mean he was safe, and she would do well to remember it.

Jessa opened the sketchpad and began tearing out the sheets, spreading the designs across the tabletop.

"Photos would be better," she began, and those were the last words she got in for some time, as everyone else suddenly began talking all at once. Everyone but Garrett.

He stood with his back to the doorjamb, just watching—her, mostly—while the others gushed over her designs. Her awareness of him almost robbed her of her enjoyment of the women's praise. He distracted her so much that she had a hard time following the conversation, which was why she didn't realize she'd been asked a question until the room fell silent.

"I—I'm sorry. Say again?"

Ellie seized both of her hands. "I said, won't you come shopping with us tomorrow?"

"Shopping?"

"For dresses. We don't have a lot of time," Ellie insisted, tugging on her hands. "I need your eye. You can help me choose the right bridal gown. I know you can. Please?"

Jessa blinked and looked down at her well-worn clothing. What on earth made Ellie think that she would be any good at picking out clothes? "Oh, I don't think—"

Ellie swept up a drawing, holding it before her. "I had this in my head. Not all of it. I could never imagine all these flowers, but these colors…the shape. It's perfect! Don't you see? Garrett was right. You *get* me. Please say you'll come. We'll have such fun, I promise, just us girls."

Fun. When was the last time she'd had fun? Jessa wondered. Oh, Abby could make her laugh, and she and Hunter enjoyed a good board game from time to time, but…Hunter.

She shook her head. "My son needs me here."

"On Saturday?" Ellie protested. "You don't homeschool on Saturday, do you?"

"Well, no."

"Carol would welcome the chance to spend more time with Hunter," Magnolia said helpfully. "She's told everyone what a delight he is."

"So darling!" Odelia trilled, glancing up from one of the drawings.

"My, yes," Hypatia added. "Why, our grand-niece, Gilli…" She broke off and cleared her throat, murmuring, "Well, she is younger than he is."

"And wilder," Odelia added happily. "Much wilder." She held up the drawing, pointed to the center of the floral arrangement depicted and said, "Wouldn't this be lovely with a big blossom right here? How big do flowers get, anyway?"

A big blossom. Yes, Jessa could almost see it now. It struck her then. Big, that was the key to Odelia. Ellie was a little extra, a bit voluptuous, a tad brighter and bolder, one more color in the usual palette. Odelia was huge, all the colors all the time, gaudy, even. For the wedding, though, she would need a gossamer overlay, a touch of elegance to carry it off. Jessa couldn't resist a glance at Garrett. He was still watching her, laughter in his eyes.

"How big were you thinking, ma'am?" she asked.

Odelia put down the drawing and held up both hands, demonstrating. She wanted a blossom at least six-inches wide. Jessa tried not to smile. Yes, of course, she would.

"I'll have to do some research."

"You haven't said you'll come shopping with us tomorrow," Ellie pointed out, seizing Jessa's hands again.

"Oh, do say you'll come," Odelia pressed.

"Hunter will be fine here," Garrett said. "The house is filled with adults, after all."

She faced him, and for an instant, their gazes held as if neither could quite look away. Finally, Hypatia said, "We'll pay you, of course."

Jessa jerked around. "That won't be necessary. I'm not a fashion consultant."

"You'll go, then!" Ellie crowed, engulfing her in a hug. "Thank you, thank you, thank you!"

What could Jessa say except, "I look forward to it."

And she did. She really did. Especially, she told herself, since Garrett Willows would not be part of the company. Hunter would be safe and content here with Carol. They could play board games and watch TV, maybe take a walk around the estate.

"Now I really have to get running," Ellie exclaimed. "I don't want to be wearing tonight's dinner when I try on dresses tomorrow!"

"About the flowers," Jessa said before Ellie could step away.

Ellie turned back to the table and separated out three drawings. "These are my favorites. I'm thinking these two at the church—multiples of these two—and this one for the reception."

"All right," Jessa said. "We'll talk bouquets and boutonnières after you have the dress."

Laughing, Ellie ran out of the room. "See you all in the morning!"

Magnolia and Hypatia traded looks. Then Hypatia shared a conspiratorial smile with Jessa.

"Thank goodness," she said, leaning forward and pitching

her voice low. "Magnolia and I feared we'd be outnumbered with two brides and our niece Dallas along. You'll meet her tomorrow. She's really a dear girl, but, um…"

"She's named after our sister," Magnolia said pointedly. "Dallas Odelia Chatam."

Jessa bit her lip to hide her own smile, knowing exactly what the older woman meant. As if to underscore it, Odelia sighed, turned in a circle with the drawing she'd fixed on earlier in her hands.

"Just imagine!" she trilled. Then she stopped and gave Jessa a wide-eyed look. "Magnolias are large. Maybe I should wear a crown of magnolias in my hair. What do you think?"

Behind her, Garrett made a choking sound. Jessa managed to swallow her own laughter and stammer, "Well, I—I think it would depend on the v-veil."

"Oh. Of course." She wandered toward the door with the drawing, murmuring, "I need to add that to my list."

Garrett snagged the drawing as she drifted out of the room. She sent him a vacant smile and went on her way. Hypatia and Magnolia followed, shaking their heads and whispering together. Chuckling, Garrett carried the drawing to the table. Jessa added it to the stack that she was gathering.

"Told you that Ellie would love your ideas," he said unabashedly, sliding his hands into the pockets of his jeans. Jessa nodded, almost painfully aware of him. "You know," he drawled, "I've paid you several compliments. Would it kill you to say thanks?"

Jessa felt heat rush into her face. Why couldn't she seem to remember even the most basic etiquette when she was around this man?

"You're right. I apologize."

"Don't need an apology," he said.

"Then, thank you. For complimenting my designs. A-and for earlier with Hunter."

He pulled his hands from his pockets and loosely folded his arms. "You mean for stating the obvious, that he's a good kid?"

"No. Well, yes. But mostly for not..." She shook her head, realizing suddenly what she'd been about to reveal.

"Not?" he prodded.

She ignored the prompt, saying, "He won't bother you again. I'll see to it that he stays out of the greenhouse."

Garrett frowned, studying her like a bug under a microscope. "I told you that I don't mind him being in there."

"But he broke the pot."

"He'll be more careful next time."

"No," she said, stepping back, "it's best if he stays away."

"I don't see why," Garrett argued conversationally, stepping forward. "I like having him around, and I think he likes me well enough."

"That's why," she snapped, feeling crowded. "That is, I—I don't think it's healthy for him to form attachments that can only be temporary."

"Why should it be temporary?" Garrett asked, folding his arms, which drew attention to the breadth of his shoulders. "Granted, we won't always be living in such close proximity," he went on, "but the Chatams are not the kind who let go of friendships easily, and I sure don't have so many friends that I wouldn't welcome a couple more."

Jessa stepped around him and went to pick up the rest of the sketches from the table. "What makes you think that we'll be staying in Buffalo Creek after we leave here?"

"You're no longer interested in the Monroe place?"

She whirled around. "Of course, I am! But we both know it's going to you."

He tilted his head. "What makes you think so?"

Jessa lifted her chin and told him. "Magnolia. She's like a mother bear with her cub when it comes to you."

A wry smile curved his lips, and he shook his head. "I'm no cub, Jessa. I'm a full-grown man. I'm not ashamed to say that I'm fond of that old girl, and she's good to me. She's treated me better than anyone in my life. But she doesn't have authority over anything that has to do with me, and that includes the Monroe Place."

"What are you saying?"

He stayed silent, then finally answered, "We don't know what the future holds. All we can do is wait and see."

She couldn't argue with that, so she simply nodded as he turned and moved toward the door. Sighing, she slipped the drawings back into the sketchpad to protect them. But how, she wondered, was she going to protect herself and her son? Garrett talked of friendship, but she didn't know how to be friends with men like him or with people who lived like this. Glancing around the room, she admired the rich decor, but all she really wanted was a safe place to work and raise her son.

How safe could they be, she asked herself, with Garrett around, tempting them to trust. Tempting her to hope. Tempting her to care.

Turning the vase slowly, Garrett tried to see with Magnolia's eyes. She had come to the greenhouse early to arrange the parlor flowers before the big shopping expedition. She had a deft hand with this sort of thing and took great satisfaction in not only arranging but growing the flowers that she used. Still, she could learn a thing or two from Jessa, and she knew it.

"I can be of help with the wedding flowers, don't you think?" Mags asked, poking stems into holes that only she could see.

"Of course, you can," he answered heartily. "I'm sure Jessa would welcome your assistance."

"So, just how much do you like Jessa?"

He had to struggle not to show his surprise and discomfort. He should have known that Magnolia would notice the undercurrent between him and the lovely Ms. Pagett, but he hadn't been prepared for her bald-faced question.

"I like her fine. She's bit a skittish, a little too private, even a little prickly, but she's a good mother and a top-notch florist, judging by her designs."

"I think she's hiding from someone."

He dropped a pair of garden shears, shocked that Magnolia had figured that out. Thankfully, it gave him an excuse to stoop and hide his face from her.

"Oh? What makes you say that?"

"Lots of little things. Don't pretend you haven't noticed them."

He sighed mentally, and met frankness with frankness. "I think the boy's been abused somehow."

Mags worked for several moments, plucking droopy petals here and there before saying sadly, "That would explain why Hunter is so docile."

"More like frightened," Garrett corrected.

Hunter had even been frightened of *him,* and so had his mother. They still were, to some extent. The thought made Garrett's chest tighten.

Magnolia stepped back and wiped her hands on the apron that she wore over her ubiquitous shirtwaist. "I have to run. The girls will be ready to leave. Could you tidy up here and put these in the parlor for me?"

"Of course."

She patted his cheek and hurried out. He spent some time cleaning the workbench. The better part of an hour passed before Garrett carried the enormous flower arrangement into the house. As he passed through the foyer, he saw the boy sitting glumly on the bottom step of the staircase.

"Hey," he said.

"Hey."

He walked on. After placing the flower arrangement, he returned to find the boy right where he'd left him.

"What's up?" he asked, leaning against the newel post.

"Nothin'," came the gloomy answer.

"Waiting for your mom?"

Hunter nodded.

"Could be some time before she returns, you know."

"Yeah."

"Okay. Well, where's Carol?"

"Kitchen. For a 'mergency."

"I see. Wait here a minute, okay?"

Hunter nodded again. Garrett walked down the hall and pushed open the kitchen door. Hilda and Carol were on their knees mopping up something red from the floor.

"Don't come in!" Hilda ordered. "I dropped an open gallon can of tomato sauce."

"I'll just take Hunter along with me, then," Garrett volunteered.

"He won't be any trouble," Carol told him gratefully.

"Yes, I know," Garrett said, leaving them to it.

He returned to Hunter and, as he'd seen Jessa do several times, reached down an open hand. The boy stared at that hand, not quite sure of it.

"Want to help me trim some topiaries?" Garrett asked. Hunter just looked at him. "Want to *watch* me trim some topiaries? You don't have to do anything, but it'll be better than sitting here staring at the door." Still the kid hesitated. "I'd like you to come. I like having a boy around, and you can come back to the house anytime you want."

Slowly, Hunter reached up and slid his hand into Garrett's.

Smiling, Garrett tugged him to his feet and led him through the house. Now, if he could just figure out how to get Jessa to take the other hand, he thought to himself, he could relax.

Except thoughts of Jessa invariably made his heart beat a little faster. He'd always found her attractive, from the very instant that he'd caught her in his arms, but the world was full of attractive women who didn't make him eagerly look forward to seeing them, getting to know them, even irritating them a little just to see them fight back.

He smiled to himself, wondering how she fared that morning. Shopping with the Chatam sisters had to be a hair-raising experience. Add Ellie and Dallas to the equation, and Garrett shuddered to think of it. Something told him, though, that Jessa could hold her own, and if she could do that then she just might enjoy herself. He hoped so, and not just for her sake. He, after all, had encouraged her to go along on the outing. If it didn't work out well, she was not going to be happy with him. The idea made his chest tighten again.

He shook his head.

How much did he like Jessa Lynn Pagett? More and more as time went by.

Chapter Six

Settling onto an armless, pink satin-covered chair with a heart-shaped seat and back, Jessa laid her sketchpad across her lap, covering a tiny pull in the fabric of her only pair of dress slacks, which she'd worn with a pale green blouse today. She felt colorless and shabby next to lush Ellie and red-headed Dallas, Asher's sister and a niece of the Chatams, but Jessa liked each of them a great deal. She felt a growing fondness for the Chatams, too.

Odelia could barely contain her enthusiasm, wiggling like a puppy expecting a treat. Hypatia, however, lent decorum to the proceedings. No pawing through crowded clothing racks for her. She had called ahead to several select Dallas shops and arranged private viewings. Magnolia brought her sturdy common sense to the proceedings, curbing Odelia's exuberance and Hypatia's overly formal demeanor.

They had been driven into Dallas in the Chatams' car by Chester, and the fawning had begun the moment that they'd walked through the door of the first shop. The shrewd proprietor had immediately sized up the group and picked out Ellie as the bride. Hypatia took it upon herself to introduce Odelia as the other bride. The proprietor, a tall, slender middle-age woman with a sleek dark chignon, never blinked an eye.

"How thrilling! Two brides in one party. Right this way, ladies." She'd placed them in pink satin chairs and whisked the brides away.

The fashion show began with Ellie, who tried on every dress in the building. Jessa was astonished that, amidst all the chatter, her quiet suggestions seemed to carry great weight. When she expressed her personal opinion that the mermaid silhouette and bateau neckline suited Ellie best, the others agreed.

"Jessa's right," Ellie decided, twisting this way and that in front of the mirrors. She now knew what she was looking for, but she did not, unfortunately, find *the* gown.

Odelia's choices were more limited, but she was thrilled to try them on. None caught her fancy, and Jessa was reluctant to give an opinion unless directly asked.

They had better luck at the second shop, where Ellie had the management hold a stunning gown for her. It was decorated with silvery gray embroidery on the bottom of the chiffon skirt and the long train, which fell from the shoulders, but the skimpy matching veil simply did not suit Ellie.

They moved on to a third and a fourth shop, where Odelia found her perfect gown, a lace-over-satin column dress that somehow managed to be both tasteful and flamboyant, thanks to an enormous organza-and-lace flower on one shoulder. In the fifth and final shop, Ellie found a long, sheer organza veil that she liked.

"What if we added silver embroidery to the edge of the veil?" Jessa suggested. "Then it would match the gown. We could anchor it with a ring of rosebuds." Ellie was delighted with the idea, so Jessa quickly sketched the pattern for the shop seamstress, who promised to have the embroidery done within forty-eight hours.

Ellie hugged Jessa, exclaiming, "You're a godsend!"

Jessa blinked back tears. No one had ever said that to her before.

To celebrate the successful shopping trip, Hypatia insisted on treating everyone to refreshments at a tearoom in an exclusive hotel. Jessa's self-consciousness returned with a vengeance, but she did enjoy the lavish high tea with its beautiful little finger sandwiches to go along with a delicious tea blend. They chattered and laughed. Jessa couldn't remember having such fun. Even her discomfort over Hypatia's insistence on saying a very public prayer of thanksgiving did not dim her enjoyment of the day. It helped that everyone gushed over her designs for the bridal bouquets, but Magnolia did have a worry.

"Where are we going to get pale lilac roses and silver filigree ribbon?"

Jessa shrugged. "I'll arrange to visit the local wholesalers. I'm sure we can order what we need."

"Why arrange a second trip into the city?" Hypatia wanted to know. "Let's just go there now."

Off to the flower markets they went. Jessa came away astonished at what the Chatam sisters ordered. In addition to the flowers, they insisted on purchasing every other material she would need to create the bouquets: stem wires and tape, fixatives and spacers, protective papers and storage boxes, ribbons, holders... When Jessa argued that she could pick up smaller quantities of the materials in retail shops, Magnolia just patted her hand and said, "Oh, but you can use the leftovers in your business, can't you?"

Jessa wanted to ask if that meant she would get the Monroe place, but she thought of Garrett and his greenhouse, and the words dissolved on her tongue. What, after all, made her any more deserving of the Monroe place than him? She simply nodded and managed a smile. The next moment, she silently scolded herself.

Garrett Willows could take care of himself. With the backing of the preeminent family in the area, he could find another place, an even better one. Her only connection was a retired schoolteacher who had been a good friend to her late mother and knew Ellie Monroe. Why, oh, why hadn't she spoken up and pressed her advantage? What was wrong with her? She should not have lost sight of what was best for her and her son just because Garrett was handsome and charming.

She'd known that man was going to be trouble. She didn't realize how much trouble, though, until their happy party returned to Chatam House.

After looking for Hunter in their suite, she went to the kitchen—and found Carol having a leisurely cup of tea at the table with her sister.

"Hunter?" she echoed in reply to Jessa's question concerning the whereabouts of her son. "Oh, he's fine. He's somewhere with Garrett."

Somewhere? With Garrett! Jessa headed for the greenhouse. She knew that she was overreacting, but she couldn't seem to help herself. What might that man have done to her son while she was gone? Why hadn't she done a better job of protecting Hunter? She had vowed never to leave her child at risk again, but the Chatams had beckoned, and off she'd gone as if she didn't have a care in the world!

To her horror, the greenhouse was empty, as was the side yard. Jessa returned to the house on the verge of panic. She went straight to the front parlor and pushed open the pocket doors. Her fear turned to knee-weakening relief when Magnolia smiled and said, "Why, they're raking the gravel beneath the porte cochere at the side of the house, dear, or so Chester says."

Jessa let out a pent-up breath, murmured her thanks and turned away. By the time she found her way through the house to the side entrance, however, relief had morphed into blazing anger.

How dare Garrett just take charge of her son? How dare he? Wasn't it enough that he had turned all her plans upside down, then made her imagine foolish little romantic scenarios just as if her heart had never been broken? Suddenly it seemed as if Garrett Willows was to blame for all the woes in her world, and she'd be hanged if she'd let him get away with it.

"Good job," Garrett said, patting Hunter on the shoulder. The boy smiled up at him, holding his rake by the end.

"It's all level again," he remarked proudly.

"It is."

Garrett periodically raked the gravel to keep it from rutting and disappearing into the grass. From time to time, Chester brought up the idea of paving the great looping drive with concrete, but Garrett agreed with the Chatams that the gravel seemed more natural, given the age of the mansion, which had been built in 1860. Today's exercise had been more about keeping a little boy busy than anything else, though.

Hunter was quiet and cooperative—unlike Gilli Leland, the young daughter of Reeves Leland, another Chatam nephew, both of whom had stopped by that day—but Garrett had seldom had a busier day than this one. He appreciated those long-ago days when he'd tagged along after his dad all the more now. What patience Matthew Willows had possessed!

The door opened, and Garret glanced toward the square stoop, finding Jessa there. Surprisingly, he hadn't heard the car arrive. He smiled, but it quickly died. Anger sparked in

Jessa's dark eyes. Sighing inwardly, he reached for Hunter's rake just as the boy bounded up the steps to hug his mother.

"Mommy! We cut the toperies!"

"Topiaries," Garrett corrected halfheartedly.

"And there's a soccer ball to kick and a big TV for games," Hunter hurried on, more animated than Garrett had ever seen him. "And a girl came to play."

"Gilli Leland," Garrett put in. "Great-niece of the Chatams."

Hunter screwed up his face and pointed at the giant magnolia tree in the side yard. "She says you can knock cats out of the tree, and there is one. It's real ugly, but I didn't knock it down. I just threw the rocks softly. Garrett said it was okay."

"Hunter was very patient and careful with Gilli," Garrett said proudly. "She's younger than him and, well, a handful, if you get my meaning. Although, I have to admit that she's calmed down a lot since Reeves married Anna Burdett."

Jessa's eyes burned him to a crisp, but she managed a smile for her son, who rattled on without drawing breath.

"The cat is Tom Curly."

"It's a tom named Curly," Garrett corrected hastily. "Belongs to Kent."

"And they got toys in the attic," Hunter chattered. "Garrett and me made a..."

"Ferris wheel," Garrett supplied.

"With these sticks that you put in holes in these round things."

"Tinker Toys."

Garrett had been appalled to find that the boy possessed only two or three small toys, so he had asked Carol what had happened to the things Gilli had played with while she and her father were in residence after honeybees had invaded their house last year. Carol had shown them a big box of playthings in the attic. Most were decades old, but they were new to the delighted boy. Garrett hadn't been able to resist sitting down on the floor to play with him.

Hunter chattered about lunch and how he only had two cookies with a banana and milk later.

"And, boy, am I hungry now!" he declared.

"Hilda probably has another cookie for you," Garrett said with a chuckle.

Jessa opened the door and held it for the boy, saying, "Just one. I don't want you to ruin your dinner. Then run upstairs and get ready for a bath. You're too dirty for the dinner table."

Hunter acquiesced happily, but before heading inside, he ran back to Garrett and slapped hands with him. "See you later, 'gator."

"After 'while, crocodile."

Smiling, the boy ran into the house. Jessa's gaze seemed less angry now, but she was clearly disturbed about the boy spending the day with Garrett. He tried to explain.

"Carol had to help Hilda clean up an accident in the kitchen. So, I kept Hunter with me. We had a great day. He's a great kid. I really enjoyed having him around. And I hope you know that I would never, ever, do anything to hurt him. Or you."

She caught her breath at that, then said tersely, "It's best if we…if *he* doesn't become too attached to you."

"Why?"

Her pretty lips flattened into a straight line.

Garrett nested the rakes, holding both in one hand. "You're hiding from his father, aren't you? You're afraid you'll have to run again."

"His father and I are divorced, and I am Hunter's custodial parent by order of the court. That's all you need to know."

"Okay. I'm not trying to pry. I just want you to understand that you're among friends here and have nothing to fear."

"You don't the first thing about fear!" she snapped.

Not know about fear? He didn't know whether to laugh or shout. Oh, he knew fear, all right. Unrelenting fear on so many levels that resolving one did nothing to ease the mind. He opened his mouth to tell her so, but she had already turned back into the house, the door closing behind her. Garrett gnashed his teeth, wondering if that woman would ever warm up to him.

Maybe it was best this way, though. After spending the day with Hunter, Garrett very much wanted to help the boy and his mom. He'd started to wonder if maybe he wasn't supposed to do that. Then he'd started to wonder if God might even mean for him to become more to them. But that was obviously just his attraction to Jessa asserting itself. She was worlds above him. Besides, how could he become more to her when she wasn't even interested in being his friend?

No, the best thing he could do was to just keep his distance and say a prayer for the two of them every now and again.

Gulping down the painful bubble that rose in his chest, he picked up his rake and grimly faced the evening ahead.

"Well, what do you think now?" Magnolia asked, returning to her seat on the settee after once more closing the parlor doors. Everyone in the house knew not to open those doors when they were closed, everyone except Jessa.

"Ellie's right," Hypatia said with a satisfied smile, "Jessa was an enormous help today."

"You don't think she's hiding anything?"

"Oh, yes, I think she's hiding *something.* Hunter did tell Carol that he wasn't supposed to talk about his last name, after all."

"I wonder if she's not hiding *from* something," Magnolia suggested. "Or, rather, hiding from *someone.*"

"Like who?" Odelia wanted to know.

Magnolia sighed. "I asked Abby Streeter about her, and all she would say is that Jessa and the boy had had a rough time of it but that things had gotten better since the divorce. Garrett thinks they were abused."

"Ah," Hypatia said. "That makes terrible sense."

"It's so sad," Odelia opined. "Marriage is supposed to be forever."

"I doubt she had a choice except to divorce, dear," Hypatia said soothingly. "I agree that she and the boy were almost certainly abused. Surely, you've noticed how she tries to fade into the background and hold herself aloof. She seems wary, as if she's expecting everyone to turn on her at any moment, and look at how timid the child is."

Odelia's face clouded. After a moment she asked, "Doesn't that remind you of someone?"

Magnolia nodded. "Garrett, once upon a time."

"Then perhaps he is the one best suited to minister to her," Hypatia mused. "God must have meant that when He brought her here."

"Or He meant *her* for Garrett," Magnolia stated baldly.

Odelia gasped. "Do you really think so?"

Magnolia stroked her braid with both hands. "I've known for a while that the time has come for him to move on with his life. He should be out on his own, building a real life for himself, not stuck here catering to three old ladies."

"Oh, but that would mean three weddings to plan!" Odelia rhapsodized. "What fun!"

"Now, now," Hypatia warned, "we mustn't run ahead of God. Matters of the heart belong to Him. Our job is to share our home and His love with others as He brings them to us. I mean, we can't expect every houseguest's visit to turn into a romance."

"So true," Magnolia agreed.

But she knew what she knew. She'd seen the way Jessa and

Garrett looked at each other, especially when they thought no one else was paying attention. She kept that to herself, though. The last thing she wanted was Odelia gushing to everyone about a possible romance between Garrett and Jessa.

Odelia proved her sister's caution warranted when she sighed dreamily and said, "Oh, what a handsome groom Garrett will make. Almost as handsome as my Kent."

Kent Monroe handsome? Magnolia thought. With his balding head, shaggy eyebrows and huge belly? Love truly was blind, Magnolia decided. She shared a guilty glance with Hypatia and bit her lip. It wouldn't do for Odelia to wonder about her smile.

"I don't know," she managed after a moment, "now that I think of it, if her first marriage was unhappy, Jessa might not wish to remarry. And surely God has someone more… trusting in mind for Garrett."

"Hmm," Odelia said, her romantic illusions depressed. At least for the moment.

Sending Magnolia a resentful glance, Garrett sized up his options then slipped into the chair next to Hunter at the dinner table. By sitting next to Hunter, he avoided a seat directly across the table from Jessa. His hide still smoked from their encounter earlier, though she had kept her anger carefully banked. Nevertheless, Magnolia had insisted that he join the family for dinner again that evening, and she hadn't been interested in his reasons for not wanting to do so. He asked himself what had gotten into the womenfolk around here. One little shopping trip and they all came back breathing fire!

Hunter smiled up at Garrett, his lips curving into silent welcome. Softening, Garrett wondered what it would take for that boy to show some teeth and smiled himself at the idea of it. Ellie hurried into the room, talking a mile a minute.

"You won't believe the dresses we bought! Jessa is so good. She has the most exquisite taste."

What followed was a fifteen-minute monologue by Ellie on the day's shopping expedition. Odelia proved surprisingly mum, saying only that she wanted to "wow" Kent on their big day.

"My darling, you 'wow' me every moment of every waking hour," he told her indulgently.

"Sugar, you haven't seen anything yet," Ellie quipped, winking at Odelia, who giggled like a schoolgirl.

Magnolia cleared her throat and addressed Hunter. "So, young man, how was your day?"

"Super!" Hunter answered instantly. Then, to the surprise of every adult at the table, he launched into a detailed description of all that he and Garrett had done that day.

"I couldn't use the scissor-thingies," he said, meaning garden shears, "but I showed him where to cut to make it twisted, and then he got the soccer ball, and I can kick it! Really, I can. And we had games on the big TV. Cool, huh?" He wrinkled his nose then. "I'm not very good."

"You did well for your first time," Garrett insisted.

Hunter flashed him a smile and went on and on about it being okay to throw pebbles at the tree that didn't really have cats growing in it and playing with "Tinky Toys" and Gilli chasing him through the rose arbor and...

"All right, son," Jessa interrupted quietly. "That's enough."

"No, no, we're enjoying his conversation," Hypatia said, calmly eating her dinner.

Hunter shifted in his chair and ate a green bean before suddenly bursting out with, "You got to rake the gravel up on the sides then straight down, like, in a row! And the attic's not dusty at all, even if Carol said we'd find bunnies there. Garrett says maybe they'll ride the fairy whirl when we're sleeping tonight."

"Fairy whirl?" Odelia asked in hopeful confusion.

Garrett quietly explained about the Ferris Wheel built of Tinker Toys on the attic floor and the imaginary dust bunnies.

"Oh, what fun!" Odelia exclaimed, clapping her hands.

"Yeah, lots of fun," Hunter confirmed, looking at Garrett with shining eyes.

Chuckling, Garrett bumped the boy's shoulder with his elbow and again he got that tight-lipped smile. *Some day,* Garrett told himself, *I'm going to see those teeth!* But the next instant he realized that it might not be so. This, in fact, might be his last chance to see the kid happy. Jessa would probably keep Hunter away from him after this because she obviously considered him a bad influence. Maybe if he told her that he would drop his claim to the Monroe place, she'd look on him more kindly. Then again, perhaps she wasn't so wrong about him.

He comforted himself with the idea that at least she didn't know the worst. Perhaps she never would, for after she left Chatam House, whether to go to the house on Charter Street or elsewhere, she obviously had no intention of ever seeing him again.

The remainder of the dinner conversation focused on weddings. Ellie announced that her only attendants would be Dallas and Petra Chatam, Asher's sisters. Asher's brother, Phillip, and cousin, Chandler, would stand up with him. Odelia and Kent opted for her sisters. Period. Hypatia, predictably, reacted negatively.

"But…Kent can't stand at the altar *unattended!*"

Kent cleared his throat, dabbed his mouth with his napkin and looked straight to Magnolia. "I was hoping that Magnolia would stand with me."

"And you could be my maid of honor," Odelia said to Hypatia. "That way you'd both have positions of honor."

"Nothing says Grandpa must have a male attendant," Ellie put in helpfully, clearly pleased. "I mean, this is the twenty-first century. Right?"

Magnolia glanced around the table then started to laugh. "I guess that makes me the best maid!"

Hypatia blinked, swallowed and muttered, "Why do I feel like a relic?" Garrett looked down to hide his smile, but Kent chuckled fondly. Hypatia sighed. "Well, I suppose if I can be a maid of honor at my age—" Realizing that she trod upon shaky ground, she shot a glance at Odelia, straightened and said, "It's not my wedding, it's yours, and of course you should do as you wish."

Odelia beamed. Ellie clapped. Magnolia laughed again. Kent nodded gratefully to his "best maid."

Garrett marveled at the delight in triplicate that was the Chatam sisters. How blessed he was to know and work for them. After the long years of darkness, God had placed him squarely within the light and love of Chatam House. And now He had done the same for Jessa and Hunter. He could only pray that Jessa realized what a blessing it was to be here. Meanwhile, Garrett determined not to feel sorry for himself. As Hypatia said, in mourning the lack of one blessing a person could easily fail to have gratitude for another. Whatever happened, he was determined not to fail in gratitude.

After the meal, the diners went their separate ways. Ellie hurried off to call Asher. He'd had a dinner meeting that evening, and they'd apparently been out of touch as long as they could bear. Tonight all the lovey-dovey stuff depressed him, however. When Kent and Odelia went off to sit in the rose arbor together, cooing like turtledoves, he actually felt a moment of irritation. Then Hypatia said something about needing a long, hot bath, and he realized that he was not the only one feeling out of sorts tonight.

Poor Hypatia, she'd done her best to adjust to the changes

that the Monroes had brought to Chatam House. Magnolia, on the other hand, seemed to have flourished, gaining new energy for this next phase in her life. She took Jessa and Hunter to investigate the toy situation in the attic.

Garrett found himself wandering restlessly to the kitchen, where he made a cup of sweet mint tea, which he carried out to the patio. The night could not have been more mild. The air brushed against his skin with the whisper softness of warm silk, and a pale, perfect half-moon hung high overhead in a navy blue sky slowly deepening to black. Garrett chose a chaise longue just outside the circle of light cast by a hanging lantern and settled upon the cushions, sipping his tea and listening to the faint music of the fountain that flanked the patio.

After years of regimented chaos, he treasured these precious moments of sublime simplicity. He opened his mind to God and drank in tranquility with his tea. Peace gradually filled him.

He remembered a verse from Luke, chapter twelve.

Do not be afraid, little flock, for your Father has been pleased to give you the kingdom.

Inhaling deeply, Garrett whispered a prayer into his cup, thanking God for this little kingdom of peace and the many riches of His greater kingdom. It was enough. If God so deemed it, how could it not be?

He didn't know how long he'd sat there, basking in the serenity, when the door opened off the sunroom, and he turned his head to see Jessa stepping through it. Surprised, he swung his feet off the chaise and down to the ground, pivoting sideways on the cushion. She ducked her head, smiling sheepishly, a worried expression clouding her dark eyes. He knew

at once that she had come to mend fences, and his heart leapt
with joy.

Never, he told himself silently, *underestimate God's willingness to give peace to His children.*

Chapter Seven

"Hello," she greeted him softly.

"Hi."

Smiling wryly, she nodded at his cup. "Are you drinking tea?"

He gave the mug in his fist a bemused glance. "Yeah. The stuff kind of grows on you after a while." He made a show of looking behind her and asked, "Where's Hunter?"

"He's in the attic with Magnolia picking out which toys he wants to keep for his own."

"Ah. Had a feeling that would happen. Actually, I'm surprised Mags didn't just run out and buy him a bunch of new stuff."

Jessa laughed soundlessly. "She did suggest that, but I put my foot down."

No surprise there, Garrett thought, though he wisely refrained from saying so.

An awkward silence ensued. Suddenly, Garrett realized that he was being rude and popped up to his full height, he waved his cup at the chaise. "Sorry. Want to sit?"

She shocked him by nodding then walking over to gingerly lower herself onto the very cushion that he had just vacated. She sat sideways on the chaise, her feet flat on the brick of the patio. Garrett managed to maintain a normal expression as he sat next to her.

"I, um…I think I overreacted this afternoon," she told him hesitantly.

Something inside Garrett loosened. Chuckling, he said, "I've never known anyone who could be so mad without exploding."

She took a small breath, as if she might explain, but then instead she said, "Everyone here has been so good to us. It's just that…he's my son, and it's my job to protect him."

"Which you do very well," Garrett told her, choosing to ignore the implication that he might be a danger to the boy.

"Not always," she said, shaking her head. "If I had done a better job, he wouldn't be so…"

"Let me tell you something about fatherless boys," Garrett said gently. "They have a hard time figuring out what their role is, but it's the women in their lives who convince them that they can be successful men. Or not."

"And your mom did that for you," she surmised.

He saw the shock on her face when he shook his head. "No. Mom was too lost after my dad died to help even herself. I was seven when he died in a cave-in while digging a ditch. Trying to be the man of the house, I went out looking for work with an old lawnmower, and Magnolia was the only one who would hire me. More importantly, she spent time talking to me. She's the one who made me feel useful and praised the little things I did, then showed me how to do better. She's the one who talked to me about Jesus. She's the one who convinced me I could do more and be better than I believed, that I could rise above my situation and live a life of meaning and purpose. Kind of like you do with Hunter."

Jessa blinked at that, her eyes dark liquid in the moonlight. "Do you think so?"

"I know so. I've seen it."

She looked down at her hands, whispering, "I worry about not protecting him."

"Sweetie, if anything, you're a little overprotective," Garrett told her honestly, "but that's better than the opposite. Believe me."

"Didn't your mom protect you?" Jessa asked.

"She did the best she could," Garrett told her, "but she wasn't the best at setting boundaries. The truth is that I pretty much ran wild after my dad died. There were whole days when she didn't know where I was, and what kept me on the straight and narrow was the fear of disappointing Magnolia."

"No wonder you're so fond of her," Jessa said.

"Oh, I'm more than fond of her," he admitted. "I owe her so much. She has a kind of strength that my mother never did. You have it, too."

Jessa flashed him a surprised look. It was true, though. He saw it very clearly, and it gave him hope for her and Hunter. He prayed that he could help her trust that strength and pass it on to her son, just as Mags had done for him.

"I was seventeen when my mom remarried," Garrett said carefully. "I didn't know Doyle very well, but my dad had been gone for nearly ten years, so I was happy for her. Then one morning I walked into the kitchen and she had a bruise in the shape of a handprint around her throat."

Jessa gasped, her hand going to her own throat.

"Of course, Mom had an explanation," Garrett related softly, "for that bruise and the next and the next."

Jessa bowed her head.

"I tried to stand up for her," Garrett said, "but she'd always get between Doyle and me. One day we got into a shouting match, and he told me to get out. I begged her to come with me, but she just kept saying that he was her husband." Jessa sighed, so he asked, "Any of this sound familiar?"

For a long moment, Jessa said nothing. Then she nodded

and whispered, "I married too young, didn't know anything about men."

Garrett's heart began a slow, pronounced beat. Here was his chance to help her. He didn't know why it was so important that he do so, but she was finally opening up, and he meant to make the most of this opportunity. He chose his words with care.

"How could you know anything about men? Your dad had walked out when you were very young."

She tilted her head back, gazing up at the night sky. "For a long time I thought it was my fault that my father left." She dropped her gaze to her hands. "He'd yelled at me for arguing with my sister. Then he grabbed his keys and said he was going to the store. He never came back."

Garrett resisted the urge to squeeze the dainty hands that she knotted together atop her knees, saying instead, "Oh, man. What a rotten thing to do. And you carried that into your marriage."

"I guess. At first, I believed that Wayne got so upset with me because I was doing something wrong."

"But you couldn't placate him, could you?"

"Never," she confessed, shaking her head.

"But you stayed, trying to do better," Garrett surmised.

"I didn't think I had a choice. You see, I got pregnant right after we married."

Garrett nodded, then quietly asked, "When did he start hitting you?"

He felt her struggling to let go of the secret. Keeping the secret became a habit, he knew, a habit layered in shame. Even he had been guilty of it. He hadn't let on to anyone what had been going on inside of his mother's house, not until it was too late.

Finally, she gathered her courage and answered him in a

small, shaky voice. "I was about seven months along with Hunter."

Garrett wrestled his anger into submission. "What changed?" Garrett asked after a moment, truly needing to know. Jessa, after all, had gotten out of her situation. His mother never had. "Why did you finally decide you could leave?"

"One day he hit Hunter in public," Jessa said simply.

Garrett fought the urge to growl at the idea of someone actually striking the boy, but she spoke so softly that he was afraid he'd miss something if he didn't stay silent.

"It was the last day before Thanksgiving vacation," she went on, "and Wayne went to pick up Hunter early from school because we were going to my sister's and he didn't want to drive after dark. The teacher realized Hunter had left behind a decoration that he'd made for his aunt, so she went out to take it to him. She saw Wayne hit Hunter in the chest with his fist and knock him across the hallway. Hunter said later that it was because he hadn't been ready when Wayne came for him. The school reported the incident. Wayne was arrested. I got a protection order and filed for divorce."

"Had he hit Hunter before?" Garrett asked in a strangled voice.

"Yes, but I wasn't aware of it at the time. He'd shaken Hunter in my presence, grabbed him by the arm and the back of the neck, and he would yell right in Hunter's face, but I always intervened. We had some of our worst fights because of it. Then Wayne would show Hunter my bruises later and tell him it was his fault. I tried to tell him that it wasn't, but I knew Hunter didn't believe me. When Wayne started hitting him, he'd pick a place where it didn't easily show, knowing Hunter would keep quiet about it. Same thing he did with me."

Garrett closed his eyes, his hand gripping the tea mug

so hard he feared it might shatter. "Why didn't you leave sooner?" he croaked out.

She sighed as if she'd known that was coming. "No money. No car. And he constantly threatened to kill my mother if I went to her."

"I'm so sorry," Garrett whispered, not sure if he was speaking to Jessa or his late mom.

"I was planning to leave him when it all blew up," Jessa went on. "My mom died of a heart attack a few months prior to that, and she'd left my sister and me a little money and her shop supplies. I managed to get my share squirreled away without Wayne knowing about it, and I'd spoken to a lawyer. Then once he was in jail, I saw my chance." She smiled wanly, adding, "I've been telling Hunter ever since that he got us out."

"That's good," Garrett told her sincerely. "I'm glad you've done that."

"Me, too," she whispered before going on with her story. "When I realized that Wayne would never leave us alone, even after the divorce and all the police stuff, I moved to another town, but he found us and went to the school to try to talk to Hunter. So, I moved again, and I kept Hunter out of school, teaching him myself, but Wayne went to my sister, and she let it slip where we were. I was trying to figure out where to go next and how to get there when I remembered that I'd promised my mother I'd stay in touch with Abby. I called her, and she insisted on coming to get us. I packed up what I could, and we came here. A few days later she introduced me to Ellie."

"And you thought all your problems were solved," Garrett surmised, shaking his head.

"For about three hours."

They shared a wan smile over that, and suddenly Garrett couldn't seem to breathe. Her dark eyes held his as if they were tethered, but he was keenly aware of her lips just inches from his own. He felt the dregs of his tea slosh in the bottom of his cup and realized that he had actually reached for her. At the last instant, he made his hand turn and dashed the contents of his cup onto the ground, then he quickly edged away, leaning on one elbow to put distance between them.

He hoped that it came off like a casual action, and apparently it had because she crossed her legs and asked in a conversational tone, "What do you think is going to happen with the Monroe place?"

He dropped his gaze to his empty cup, saying, "I think you'll be setting up shop there before Odelia's wedding."

"I don't know," Jessa said with a shake of her head. "It's perfect for your purposes. Even I can see that."

"Yours, too," Garrett remarked. "Pity we can't share it."

Even as she laughed, he sat up straight. That would be the perfect solution! Why not share it?

She rose to her feet, slid her hands over the sleeves of her pale green blouse and said, "Well, I need to get back to Hunter. I just wanted to thank you for looking after him today. I didn't mean for things to work out like that, and I'll make sure it doesn't happen again."

"It was no problem," he told her, getting up belatedly. "I enjoyed the day."

"Still," she said, moving to the door. There she paused, looked back and added wistfully, "It's for the best."

With that, she went inside, leaving him to drop down onto the chaise once again. So much for his perfect solution, he thought glumly. Maybe she didn't hate him, as he'd feared, but she would never agree to share the property with him. She obviously still intended to keep him as far away as possible.

After all that she'd been through, he couldn't really

blame her. He disliked being kept at arms' length by her far more than was healthy for his heart.

Swiftly crossing the tile floor of the sunroom, Jessa acknowledged a sense of disquiet. She'd been mad to seek out Garrett tonight and reveal so much to him, but she'd also been unfair to him when she'd returned to the house earlier that afternoon and had needed to remedy that somehow.

She couldn't explain it, really. After Wayne, she'd promised herself that she would never again apologize to a man, but sitting there on the attic floor with Magnolia and Hunter after dinner, she'd watched her son's shining face as he'd gingerly turned the "fairy whirl" and she'd known Garrett was responsible for Hunter's happiness. Suddenly she hadn't been able to let another moment go by without making amends. Leaving Hunter, under Magnolia's supervision, to agonize over which three toys he would choose for his own from the overflowing toy trunk, Jessa had headed for the greenhouse, only to find Garrett sipping tea on the patio.

His obvious contentment had struck her. She'd never seen her ex-husband in so relaxed a pose. He'd either oozed charm, which she had come to realize was calculated, or perched on the precipice of violence, a predator looking for any sign of weakness. As for her long absent father, Jessa remembered him as being edgy, distant and easily irritated.

Garrett was not like either of the men from her past. But she was starting to think that he might be a genuinely good guy. Hunter certainly thought so. He had sung Garrett's praises from the moment she'd returned to the house that afternoon. So far as her son was concerned, Garrett Willows hung the moon. And what a moon it was.

Jessa smiled, recalling the perfect, pale yellow, half circle overhead. She'd never seen such a large half-moon or so clear a sky. The romance of it had unnerved her a bit, and she could only hope that Garrett hadn't noticed. An odd feeling of intimacy had enveloped them as they'd talked, and perhaps that had induced her to say more than she normally would have about her past.

Garrett had seemed to believe all that she'd said, but then he had experience with abuse himself, if what he'd told her about his mother and stepfather was true. Guilt for doubting him flashed over her, but really, how could she know? She'd taken as fact every word that Wayne had spoken to her—until he'd shown her his true self. She dared not trust her instincts where Garrett was concerned, which meant that putting distance between him and her and her son remained the only sensible option.

But what if Garrett was all that he seemed? She could be passing up the best thing that had ever happened to her. No, that couldn't be right. Hunter was the best thing ever to happen to her. It struck her suddenly that Hunter would grow up one day and make his own life, as he should. What kind of man would he be? Shy and careful? Bold and confident? Thoughtful and wise? Or some combination of all those things? And what of her? Clinging and dependent, afraid to love or be loved by anyone other than the son whom she had held too close?

She wished for the pounding of Mr. Bowen's hammer to distract her thoughts, but the Chatam sisters did not allow him to work on weekends, let alone evenings. Stepping up onto the landing, she noticed that the door to the suite stood open and that the light in the sitting room shined through the doorway. She went there and found Magnolia sitting on the couch with Hunter, listening intently while he pointed out all the details of his favorite toy car. They both looked up and smiled at her.

"Mommy, look!" Hunter cried, hopping up to run to the desk, where he had left his chosen toys.

Jessa walked over and nodded at the scarred action figure, battered toy dump truck and several sections of miniature racetrack and connectors. "Looks like fun. Did you thank Miss Magnolia?"

"He did," Magnolia confirmed, rising to walk around the sofa toward them. "I trust you found Garrett."

Jessa thought about inventing a reason for seeking out Garrett. She could always say that she wanted to talk about the flowers for the wedding, but she hated a liar and refused to become one now. That didn't mean she had to explain why she'd gone to find him. "Yes, I did."

"Very good. Well, I'll leave the two of you to enjoy your evening. We leave for church at half past nine in the morning, by the way."

Jessa wondered if attending church with the Chatams was wise. She and Hunter would be leaving soon, after all. The Chatams would surely have little time for her and her son after they left the household. Why build attachments? Besides, she doubted that she had anything to wear that wouldn't make her look like a homeless waif next to her hostesses.

"I'm not sure we can go," she said softly. "We should probably go where Abby does," she added quickly, having just thought of it. "She invited us as soon as we arrived in Buffalo Creek."

"Well, that's fine, then," Magnolia replied, beaming. "Abby attends the Downtown Bible Church the same as we do."

"I see." Jessa mentally conceded. It had been months since she and Hunter had attended church, after all. Following the divorce, she hadn't wanted to attend services where she and Wayne had gone, and without transportation, finding another church had seemed impossible. That problem had remained after she and Hunter had moved, and they hadn't been in Buffalo Creek long enough to attend a service with Abby before coming here to Chatam House.

"We'll see you in the morning, then," Magnolia said complacently. Jessa nodded. "Oh, and, I've been meaning to tell you that Carol will be happy to do your laundry for you."

"No, no, I couldn't let her do that," Jessa insisted, shaking her head.

"In that case," Magnolia told her, "you're welcome to use the washer and dryer in the laundry room. You'll find it off the covered walkway behind the kitchen between this house and the carriage house."

"Thank you. That's very helpful."

Smiling again, Magnolia left them.

Jessa sighed and brought her hands to her hips. So, it would be laundry for her tonight and church for both her and Hunter tomorrow. At least she wouldn't have to scrub their things in the bathtub.

She gathered the laundry, thinking of Garrett Willows. A man like Garrett would never be interested in her, not romantically.

Oh, he'd been friendly, helpful and kind when he'd had no reason to be any of those things. He'd spent time with her son, complimented her designs and helped her win the approval of the Chatam ladies. He'd teased her and told her about his own experience with abuse. What he had not done was flirt or entice or even touch her, since he'd caught her in his arms after she'd fallen from the ladder.

She considered that as she stuffed clothes into one of a trio of washers, going over all that Garrett had said or done, and the only conclusion depressed her. Without even realizing it, she'd started spinning romantic dreams out of nothing. How pathetic she was! She had proved Wayne right again. She was useless, at least when it came to men. That gave her all the more reason to keep her distance from Garrett. If not, she risked making an even bigger fool of herself than she had already, and she refused to be a heartbroken idiot.

Pushing Garrett from her mind, she concentrated on preparing clothing so that she and her son could attend church the following day. The last thing she wanted was for either of them, but especially him, to be self-conscious in God's house.

"He'll be all right, you know."

The sound of Garrett's voice so close by Jessa's ear had startled her, even though she had been painfully aware of him all during the ride from Chatam House to the church. To her surprise, Garrett, not Chester, had driven the town car that morning because the rest of the staff attended a different church.

Jessa turned back to the glass wall enclosing the Sunday School room to see a teacher gently urge Hunter to join a group of children coloring at a table. He waved a little, and gave a shadow of a nervous smile before allowing himself to be ushered to a chair at the table. She smiled, turning away from the window and back to Garrett.

"I know. Hunter will do fine. He's a little shy is all."

Slipping a hand into the outside pocket of her small handbag, she brushed her fingertips over the colored tag with which she would reclaim her son. The attendant at the door of the children's Sunday School suite had assured her that only the bearer of that tag, the twin of which was clipped to the belt loop of Hunter's blue jeans, could pick up her son after the service.

"You'll be fine, too," Garrett assured her, nudging her down the hall with a hand placed against the small of her back. Jessa felt his touch all the way to the marrow of her bones. "Magnolia asked me to point the way to the ladies'

Bible Study since you seemed reluctant to join her and her sisters," he explained.

"It's not that I'm reluctant," Jessa said, though it was. She knew that she and Hunter should attend church regularly, but her marriage had left her with more than one kind of bitterness.

She couldn't really blame the pastor or the other churchgoers where she had attended with Wayne for thinking that he was a man of stellar character because he hid his true self so well. Nevertheless, it had been her church, too, so she had expected support and encouragement when the truth had come to light. Instead, she had been avoided and viewed with suspicion, as if she had fooled them, too. Still, it had hurt. Churches, however, were not all the same. Rather like men.

She shook her head and said, "It's just strange."

"Hopefully not for long," he replied.

Nodding and shrugging at the same time, she let him steer her through the hallways.

"Listen," he said, "I heard Hypatia warn you that they 'eat simple' on Sundays, and I thought perhaps I ought to explain that."

"I did wonder what it meant," she confessed.

"They don't want the staff working on this day of rest, you see, so Hilda usually puts up something on Saturday, and the Chatam sisters get it on the table themselves and clean up afterward. Even Kent pitches in. I, however, am strictly forbidden." He grinned as if that pleased him mightily. Jessa couldn't help smiling in response.

They turned a corner and came to a door. "Here it is," he said, "the Esther class. I'll meet you after and walk you to the sanctuary for worship," he promised.

Jessa went in to find that the Bible study was just about to get underway. After a warm welcome, Jessa found that she enjoyed the discussion. An hour later, she filed out of the room in the midst of a dozen or so other women in her general age range to find Garrett waiting for her.

"Well?"

She had to smile. "Very well, thank you."

He chuckled. "This way."

They ambled toward the sanctuary, a soaring masterpiece of white stucco, stained glass, dark wood and brass. Much larger than the spare, plain space in which she was used to worshiping, the church made Jessa feel even more small and humble than usual. Garrett edged into an already crowded pew, making softly spoken introductions.

Hub was the elder brother of the triplets and a retired minister. His daughter Kaylie and her husband, Stephen Gallow, nodded at Jessa with open curiosity, while Reeves Leland, a nephew, and his wife, Anna, complimented Hunter's patience with their daughter, Gilli. Everyone moved over to make room, but eleven bodies were crammed onto what proved to be a ten-person pew. Garrett lifted an arm and draped it about Jessa's shoulders in an obvious effort to ease the crowding for everyone.

When Abby waved to her, Jessa considered moving. "Maybe I should sit with Abby," she whispered, but Garrett shook his head.

"It'll be just as crowded there."

Jessa stayed where she was. She had trouble concentrating at first, pressed so closely to Garrett's side, but gradually she relaxed, and as the pastor delivered his message, she began to apply it to herself.

Worry was useless, he said. So, why worry when she and Hunter were in a secure, comfortable place? Grow where you are planted, he said. Neither staff nor family, she realized that she need not be only a guest at Chatam House, either. She could help out, starting with lunch today, then she'd look for other ways to lend her aid, so that when the time came to part, she would not feel terribly beholden and the inevitable parting would be that much easier. Wouldn't it?

Chapter Eight

Jessa rose encouraged at the end of the service, convinced that she could contribute to the household and still maintain enough emotional distance that she wouldn't be hurt when these friendships faded away. When Hunter ran to her at the door of the small chapel where his age group worshiped, he happily waved a farewell to new friends, inducing Jessa to drop to her knees and hug him. They would be fine without Garrett and the Chatams, she assured herself, but Hunter had more immediate concerns.

"I'm hungry!" he announced loudly, eliciting chuckles from Garrett who had again shown Jessa the way.

Once they arrived back at Chatam House, Jessa hurried to change her clothes and get to the kitchen, where she joined the sisters in putting the midday meal on the table. The food did not disappoint. Hunter approved heartily. She allowed him to go off to the family parlor with Garrett to play video games while she helped the Chatams clean up. Then she and her son quietly excused themselves and went upstairs. They took supper, prepared by Jessa herself from the lunch leftovers, in their suite.

The afternoon and the evening passed sedately, as it had for months now, with just her and Hunter to entertain themselves. No walking on eggshells. No guarding against a volatile outburst. Yet, for the first time, a strange restlessness marred Jessa's enjoyment of their hard-won peace. She told herself that it would pass, that she was merely anxious to move into their own place. The restlessness followed her to bed, however, where she tossed and turned for hours, not worrying, not even thinking, really. Still, she could not relax.

Rising, finally, she drew on jeans and a simple T-shirt, then went out in her bare feet, leaving the door to the suite open, to wander the darkened house silently. She found no rest in any of the rooms, and her thoughts naturally turned to the greenhouse with all its flowering beauty. Suddenly, she craved the smell and feel of growing things. Wondering if Garrett left the greenhouse unlocked, she slipped outside and across the artfully broken paving.

The door swung open at her touch, and she stepped inside. Utter blackness enveloped her, but after a few moments, her eyes began to adjust. She made out the shapes of the potted trees well enough to pass through them. Humidity misted the darkened glass walls and raised dampness on the back of her neck. Sweeping the long fall of her heavy hair over one shoulder, she moved through the plants until she reached the workbench where Hunter had broken the pot. Standing motionless in the small space, she breathed deeply of the flowery perfume.

Suddenly, a black shape resolved out of the night. She knew instantly who it was and realized with dismay that he had drawn her like a lodestone.

"I'm not the only one who couldn't sleep, it seems," Garrett said softly.

She shook her head, but her feet refused to budge, even as she made her excuses. "I—I didn't mean to disturb you. I didn't know anyone would be in here."

"Come and join me," he said.

She sensed movement, then a hand appeared, faint in the darkness. Her own hand rose to meet it. Strong fingers grasped her smaller ones, his big palm cupping hers. His hand tugged, and she was lost, her feet following.

She spied a pair of plastic five-gallon buckets turned on end with a board placed atop them to form a bench. Chuckling, Jessa allowed herself to be seated. He sat down next to her, their backs to the glass walls.

"I come here at night sometimes," he told her, "to smell the earth and the plants. It soothes me."

She shot him a surprised glance, but the room was too dark to make out more than the dim silhouette of his profile.

"I understand," she said and heard his smile.

"I know you do."

He breathed in deeply, letting the air out in a long, slow sigh. "Feel that," he whispered. "Life all around us."

"Yes."

"I missed it so much," he whispered so softly that she wasn't sure she'd understood him correctly.

He leaned his head back against the glass and closed his eyes. After a moment, she did the same. Her soul quieted, and her muscles relaxed. She felt the life that Garrett had spoken of earlier and something more, a belonging, a likeness, a sense of being in the right place. She wondered if she ought to stock more potted arrangements in her shop and envisioned a series of carefully chosen plant combinations. She'd need to do some research, she decided. Her last thought as consciousness drifted away was that she could always ask Garrett.

Glancing at the pearl face of the tiny watch pinned to her lapel, Hypatia sighed. "We're going to be late if we don't leave soon."

"Are you sure she knows?" Odelia asked Magnolia. "I've hardly seen the dear girl since Sunday."

"I told Jessa myself this morning what time we would leave for prayer meeting," Magnolia reported.

"I'll find her," Garrett volunteered grimly.

Jessa had avoided the entire household like the plague ever since she'd awakened with her head on his shoulder Sunday night. He had sat there against the steamy wall of the greenhouse, listening to her even breathing and talking to God about her until his back had stiffened and ached so abominably that he'd had to shift his weight. That had awakened Jessa. He would never forget the horror on her face or how she bolted from his side. He'd chased after her, afraid to call out in the dead of night, but by the time he'd reached the greenhouse door, she had disappeared.

He sometimes wondered if he'd dreamed the whole thing. Since then, he'd caught only glimpses of her. Wherever he went, she had just left, and she never so much as acknowledged his knock upon the door of her suite, even when he knew that she was in there. Most galling of all, she'd kept Hunter out of his sight, too.

Turning for the kitchen, he strode down the hall. Hilda would know where to find Jessa if anyone did. He'd heard tales of her helping Carol clean out the linen closets and dust the attics. She'd even folded laundry and haunted Hilda in the kitchen, asking to be taught to cook and washing the dishes afterward. She was obviously attempting to earn her keep—and avoiding everyone else, him especially, in the process. Well, Garrett had had enough of being treated like a threat to her very existence, and the Chatams certainly did not deserve her behavior. It was time to get a few things straight with the lovely Jessa Lynn Pagett.

Thankfully, he didn't have to look farther than the kitchen. She stood at the sink, up to her elbows in sudsy water.

"It's fine," she was saying to Hilda. "You and Carol go on. I'll finish up here."

Hilda turned to Garrett, her pocketbook dangling from her elbow. "Since I don't have a rope to throw around her and drag her away from that sink, I guess I'll get on to the midweek meeting."

Jessa glanced around to see whom Hilda was addressing then went back to industriously scrubbing a broiler pan. Garrett smiled at Hunter, who sat at the kitchen table with a coloring book and crayons, looking woebegone and uncertain.

"Leave your things there and run out to the front door," Garrett instructed the boy calmly. Jessa whirled around, splattering the floor with dishwater. "The misses are waiting for you," Garrett went on, warning Jessa with his gaze not to interfere. "Go on with them. Your mom will come with me."

Without so much as a glance at his mother, Hunter hopped out of his chair and ran from the room. Sparks filled the air, flying between them like bullets at the O.K. Corral.

"Just where do you think you're sending my son?" she demanded once Hunter was safely out of earshot.

"Same place I'm taking you," Garrett answered. "Prayer meeting."

Her mouth flattened into a straight line. "I told Hilda I would finish—"

"Look," Garrett interrupted her, "just because you fell asleep on my shoulder, it doesn't mean anything."

"I never thought…" she said softly, averting her gaze as color warmed her cheeks. "I apologize for putting you in an uncomfortable position."

"Don't," he barked. "I wasn't uncomfortable." Well, not in the manner she meant. Disconcerted by how long he'd been willing to sit there in pain just to feel her head on his shoulder, he cleared his throat and changed tactics. "The Chatams give generously to everyone who wanders by, and they ask very little in return, only that their generosity be accepted in the same spirit in which it is given," he lectured. "They *don't* expect their guests at Chatam House to work like staff. They would take that, in fact, as an insult. If you really want to please them, you'll come along with me to prayer meeting. You see, while they pride themselves on their generosity, they'd rather know you're grateful to God than to them."

Jessa's gaze dropped like a stone in a well. "I am grateful to both," she said, turning back to rinse the pan and stack it to dry. "I just like to keep busy is all."

"Busy enough to avoid me," he snapped.

She stilled then went on with her chore, rinsing several more dishes. "I don't know what you're talking about."

"Don't you?" he asked. "Then I suppose you're working to ensure your place here at Chatam House."

"That's not what I'm doing," she insisted, shaking her head.

"Then what are you doing? Trying to fulfill some need that doesn't exist?"

She bowed her head and after a long moment said, "You're right. This is more about me not being beholden to the Chatams than filling any need here at Chatam House." She reached into the water and pulled the plug from the drain, then dried her hands on a towel as she turned to face him. "It's ungrateful and foolish," she went on softly, "and I admit that I've avoided you from embarrassment."

"There's no need for that," he told her gruffly, but still she kept her gaze averted. He swallowed and plunged on. "You never have to be embarrassed with me. Don't you know that yet? Certainly not over something so innocent."

She said nothing to that, merely set aside the towel. "Give me a moment to change."

"You're fine as you are," he told her, then abruptly added, "better wear a jacket, though. We're taking the bike."

"Bike?" she echoed.

"As in, motorcycle," he informed her, having only just decided.

A light flashed in her dark eyes, and for a heartbeat he thought that she would balk, but then her gaze hardened resolutely and she stalked past him to shove through the kitchen door. Wondering why he'd done such a stupid thing, Garrett hurried out to gather his gear and roll the bike out of the garage. She admitted to wanting to avoid him, and he forced her into even closer proximity.

Way to go, Willows, he told himself morosely.

She joined him mere moments after he pushed the bike to the front of the house. Wearing slender jeans and a short denim jacket over a simple T-shirt, her hair pulled back in a long ponytail at the nape of her neck, she looked about sixteen, young, fresh, breathtaking. He plunked the extra helmet on her head unceremoniously and fastened the chin-strap before donning his own and mounting the seat. She gingerly settled behind him. He kick-started the engine, then heeled back the stand.

"Hold on."

She didn't move a hair, so he reached back with his left hand, found her arm and pulled it around him. He revved the engine and kicked the bike into gear. At the last possible instant, her right arm banded about his waist and she leaned forward, snugging her front against his back. She could just see over his shoulder, he realized, and rode as easily on the back of his bike as if it had been fitted to her. His chest swelled with such longing that he felt the imprint of the zipper on his protective leather jacket.

He wasn't sure later how he managed to steer the bike safely to the church. The ride seemed to take seconds and, at the same time hours. Cocooned in the rushing wind, they sped through the quiet city streets. When they pushed through the chapel doors and slipped into the back pew, they were but a quarter hour late to the meeting. The music portion of the meeting had finished, but the pastor had not yet begun the Bible reading to prepare the gathering for prayer.

Drawing his Bible from an inside pocket, Garrett followed along, his concentration fierce, but when the moment for silent prayer came and he closed his eyes, he found that the words flowing from his heart were not what he'd planned. Rather than lifting up the concerns that had been listed in the distributed program and spoken aloud by those in attendance, he found his thoughts turning to selfish concerns.

Has she avoided me because she feels this attraction, too? Is she afraid or simply uninterested? Help her see how greatly I admire her strength and determination, he asked his Lord. *More importantly, if she can somehow be within Your will for me, help me deserve her.*

That was his greatest fear, really, that the mistakes of his past made him unfit for a woman of such strength, bravery and determination. He wished his mother had been more like Jessa, but perhaps she had been and he just hadn't seen it. He had longed to give her a way out of her marriage to Doyle, but had he unwittingly been the very reason she had stayed? Had she tried to protect him and his sister from her husband's brutality by staying with him? Was that why she had gone back to him time after time, even after Doyle had hospitalized her, only to die in a broken heap of bones and bruises? Because of him? Even if it hadn't been to protect him, he was still the cause of it all.

How could he think that he could ever deserve a woman like Jessa?

* * *

Folding her hands, Jessa stared down at them. When the pastor had asked for those with prayer requests to speak up, she had very nearly done so, but how could she ask others to pray that God would give her the strength not to fall in love with the man sitting next to her? How could she ask that God grant her the Monroe place so that she need not worry about making a fool of herself over him? Again.

She should never have gone into the greenhouse that night. She should never have stayed once she'd realized that he was there. She should never have let herself feel safe and comfortable with him, enough to drop off to sleep on his shoulder! She hadn't known what to say to him after that, hadn't known how to act. She still didn't. Nevertheless, she'd climbed on that bike and she'd let herself feel that she belonged there with him, if only for a little while.

What was wrong with her? A romantic complication was the last thing she needed, especially with him. He seemed to know her too well, and that horrified her.

Wayne had known her better than she'd known herself. He'd known exactly how to manipulate her, how to keep her bound to him. He'd even used her faith, her conviction that God had ordained marriage and meant it to last a lifetime. She knew Wayne had ignored his own wedding vows because he'd rubbed her nose in his infidelities, claiming that he'd strayed because of her. Already pregnant, she'd clung to her belief that God would change him.

Eventually she'd come to understand that God would not change those who did not wish to change. By then she had a child with the man, and Wayne had threatened violence to their son and even her mother to keep her at his side. Ironically, that very violence, and the small legacy left to her by her late mom, had finally allowed Jessa to escape.

She couldn't imagine that Garrett would actually harm

her, which was probably why he drew her so strongly. But how could she know? Marrying Wayne had proved how poor her judgment was in such matters. It was safer simply not to allow any man into her life. Yet Garrett Willows tempted her.

He tempted her to trust him, perhaps even to love him, and she dared not. Even if he did happen to be interested in her romantically, she dared not let herself trust that it could work out for them.

Please, Lord, she pleaded, *don't let me make the same mistake twice. I know that cannot be Your will.*

She roused herself to pray for the requests of others, those with illness and financial need, those in nursing homes and at the end of their lives. Those needs far exceeded her own, yet she continually wandered back to her concerns.

Help me be wise, she prayed at one point. *Protect me, Lord, from myself!*

By the time the meeting came to a close, Jessa felt exhausted. While she longed to ride back to Chatam House with Garrett, she knew that she should put distance between them. Why couldn't she find a way just to be his friend, especially as that was what he seemed to offer?

"An innocent thing," he'd called it, her falling asleep so easily on his shoulder. He couldn't know how many nights she'd lain awake in fear with Wayne breathing easily beside her. Or how many times her fears had been realized.

An innocent thing? No, not to her.

The Chatams greeted her warmly, and told her where to find Hunter. She hurried off to fetch her son. To her surprise, he lingered a few moments, giggling with another boy, before running to her.

"Hi, Mommy. Miss Magnolia said we might get a treat at the drive-through on the way home."

Jessa looked down at the shining, happy face of her child.

"Well," she capitulated easily, "if Miss Magnolia said so, I guess that's all right."

"Cool!"

He led her out to the foyer, babbling about his friend Tucker and the horses that he supposedly owned.

"Next year, when I get to go to real school, I can see 'em, right? 'Cause then I can go to Tucker's house and he can come to mine. When we get one. Right?"

"Right," Jessa confirmed, vowing that one way or another, she would get him a home. He would have his friends over, and she would find the courage to let him go to their homes to visit, and he would have the life he deserved, a life without fear. "Just don't let me mess it up, Lord," she whispered. "Don't let me mess it up."

They met the Chatams and Garrett on the front steps of the building. Amber lights lit the proud downtown of the graceful old city, softly illuminating the circa 1930s storefronts of the businesses that surrounded the square on three sides. The church took up the entire fourth side of the square. The ornate county courthouse, constructed of rose granite, occupied its center.

Oblivious to the grandeur, Hunter ran straight to Magnolia, all but jumping up and down in his exuberance when Chester pulled up to the curb in the town car. Garrett stood apart, holding a helmet in each hand. She waited for him to offer her one. He did not, and when Magnolia offered to bring him his favorite treat, a strawberry milk shake laced with chocolate syrup, he politely declined.

"No, no. You all go on and enjoy yourselves. I'm going to take a ride on the bike."

So, that was that, then. Jessa piled into the car with the others, but as it pulled away, she couldn't resist looking back. The sight of him standing there alone with those two helmets, his inky hair gleaming in the lamplight, made her heart turn over. He looked so strong, with those broad shoulders encased in leather, and yet oddly vulnerable. She told herself that it was her imagination. Had he wanted her to ride back with him, he'd have asked her to do so. Wouldn't he?

She told herself next that it didn't matter. She could not afford to care for him or feel more for him than mere friendship, but deep in her heart, she wished… Oh, how she wished!

That unexpressed wish followed her into sleep that night and embossed itself permanently on her heart.

Much, it seemed, as Garrett Willows himself had done.

Chapter Nine

"You're right," Jessa said to Hunter the next afternoon, flipping the textbook closed. "That's enough for today."

Hunter pushed back the desk chair and hopped out of it. "Yay! Can I go outside?"

Jessa considered his request. They hadn't seen Garrett last night after the prayer meeting or this morning at breakfast. She had to wonder who was avoiding whom now. If she let Hunter leave the house alone, though, he'd head straight for the greenhouse. Still, she couldn't keep a healthy boy cooped up in the house, not on a beautiful day in early May.

"Okay. Why don't you get the truck that Magnolia gave you? We'll go out to the rose arbor for a while."

"Cool!"

He raced off to get the toy dump truck while she tucked in the tail of her simple aqua T-shirt into her jeans. She decided to go down in her flip-flops and leave her hair caught in a ponytail at the nape of her neck. She wouldn't join the household for dinner dressed in such a fashion, but surely her outfit was adequate for playing outside.

Hunter returned with his toy, and they quickly walked down the stairs, across the foyer and out the front door. The balmy temperatures of an early summer greeted them. Sunshine as bright and clear as crystal surrounded the grace-ful old house, casting the generous porch into deep shadow. A grouping of wrought-iron furniture stood to one side of the daisy-yellow door and beyond that a white porch swing swayed lazily in a gentle breeze, inviting them to sit. Hunter missed the invitation, running across the porch and down the steps to the walkway.

Jessa followed, smiling indulgently. He left the walkway and ran across the grass toward the rose arbor, heavy with drooping red blossoms. As he drew near the flowery bower, Garrett stepped out from behind it, carrying a small, white, lacy wrought-iron bench. Bending, Garrett placed the bench beneath the arbor, then he stepped over it and opened his arms to Hunter, who literally launched himself into Garrett's embrace.

Catching her breath, Jessa stumbled. Her heart cracked at the look of delight on her son's small face. She hurried toward them, torn between following suit by flinging herself at Gar-rett and snatching her child away. In the end, she did neither.

Garrett took a seat on the bench, the boy on his knee, and ruffled Hunter's hair. "Finished your school work already?"

"Yessir. I memered all my sight words."

"Memorized," Jessa corrected automatically.

"Memorized," Hunter repeated.

Garrett chuckled. "Good for you. You'll have to read them all to me sometime."

"Okay."

Garrett looked at the battered dump truck in Hunter's hands and said, "You know what you could do with that? You could haul off all these rose petals on the ground."

"There's a bunch of them!" Hunter exclaimed, sliding off Garrett's knee.

"Yep. The roses are fading." He turned a tentative smile up at Jessa then, adding, "Roses do best with cool nights, and we've passed that time now." Nodding, she watched as Hunter scooped up the bruised, curling petals littering the ground. Garrett told him to dump them in a pail on a corner of the patio, saying that Magnolia would gather them later and use them to make sachets.

"What's sashays?" Hunter wanted to know.

"Sweet-smelling stuff," Garrett informed him. "Like what's in the gold bowl on that long table in the foyer."

"Oh. I thought that was trash."

Jessa found herself sharing a smile with Garrett over that.

"No, that's Magnolia's special recipe to keep the house smelling great."

"Huh. It works."

"Yes, it does," Garrett agreed. "I'm sure she'll appreciate your help with it."

Hunter went to work with a vengeance. Garrett moved over on the bench and addressed Jessa. "Won't you sit with me for a minute?"

Wandering over, she gingerly took a seat, keeping as much space between them as the narrow bench allowed. They sat in silence for several minutes, watching Hunter pick up petals, place them in the bed of the dump truck then drive the toy to a new spot. When the petals threatened to spill over the sides of the little truck, Hunter began driving it toward the patio with much revving of imaginary engines and shifting of gears.

After a bit, Garrett softly said, "He's a wonderful boy. You have every reason to be proud of him."

"Thank you. I am."

"It kills me to think that you might worry that I would hurt him," Garrett went on, pitching his voice lower still. "Or you."

She fought to keep her gaze from meeting his but lost. "I don't."

"I'm glad," he said, but the sadness did not leave his eyes.

They sat again in silence, until suddenly Garrett blurted, "You're not like my mom, you know. You're not desperate for some man to take care of you."

"I used to be," she admitted.

"Maybe," he conceded, "but you were young then, and you learned better. When my mother met Doyle she was worn down from years of scraping by and making do on one minimum-wage job after another. She thought he would give us financial security again, and he did. But at a very steep price." Garrett shook his head. "I could never understand why she was willing to endure his abuse just so the bills would be paid." His hand reached toward Jessa, but he quickly brought it back and sat on it, tucking it beneath his thigh. "You've given me a better perspective on that."

"What do you mean?" she asked, drawing down her brows in confusion.

"When you told me that your ex had threatened to kill your mother if you went to her, I started to think that maybe Doyle made similar threats, you know, against me and my sister."

"Abusers always look for leverage," Jessa told him.

Garrett nodded. "My stepfather had me and my sister. Your ex had your mom and Hunter."

"He used to threaten to take Hunter and disappear with him," Jessa revealed. "Once, when I pointed out that he couldn't cope with an infant, he swore he'd kill Hunter if I ever left him."

Garrett closed his eyes, a muscle working in the hollow of his jaw. Looking away, he sucked in several deep breaths. Finally, he turned back to her. "Thank you for trusting me with that information. I hope you know that I would never betray your whereabouts. I would never intentionally do anything to hurt you or Hunter. Never."

Jessa gulped. "I appreciate that."

"I hope you know, too, how much I admire you," he hurried on. "Unlike my mom, you found a way out of that abusive relationship, and you're making a life for you and your son. I'm glad for that."

Hunter ran up just then. He dropped to his knees and began gathering more petals.

"Time for a second load?" Garrett asked cheerfully, sliding off the bench and into a crouch beside the boy. "Here, let me help."

He picked up a handful of petals then cupped his hands over the bed of the truck, pretending that they were metal claws dumping a load. Hunter mimicked him, making so many metallic screeches that Jessa had to laugh. Soon the dump truck was again on its way to the patio with a full load. Garrett rose and turned, his gaze following the boy and his truck with a fond smile.

"Does Hunter swim?" he asked suddenly. "The public pool will open soon." He dropped his voice, adding softly, "I'd like to take you both to—"

"Exactly what I wanted to talk to you about!" announced a hearty voice.

Jessa looked around Garrett to find Kent Monroe trundling up from the general direction of the front of the house. She felt both disappointment and relief, disappointment because Garrett had been about to suggest an outing with her and Hunter, relief because it wouldn't have been wise. Surely, God had arranged this interruption to save her from herself.

Garrett turned to greet the other man, who pulled a folded hanky from his shirt pocket and mopped his perspiring brow. "You want to talk to me about the public pool?" Garrett asked, surprise straining his voice.

"No, no," Kent said, shaking his head so hard that his

jowls jiggled. He leaned closer to Garrett and said, "A *private* pool. Here."

"A swimming pool at Chatam House?"

"Odelia's always wanted one, you know," Kent confirmed authoritatively.

"Has she?"

Kent nodded. "Oh, my, yes. I remember that as a girl she used to beg her parents for one. They thought it would be ostentatious," he confided. "I suppose, in that era, it would have been. But now, everyone has backyard pools, and with the greenhouse moving soon, well, I thought I might have one put in just there on the other side of the patio. What do you think? Is that an appropriate wedding gift?"

Garrett cleared his throat and shot a glance at Jessa. "I'm no authority on wedding gifts, so I couldn't say, but a pool would fit nicely in that area. Have you spoken to her sisters about it?"

"Not yet. I thought I'd consult you first."

"Well," Garrett said carefully, "if they're all right with it and she wants it, I don't see why not."

"Ah," Kent said, drawing himself up so that his belly seemed to protrude even farther. "Excellent. Excellent. This is just between us, though. Yes?" He brought a finger to his lips, nodding at both Garrett and Jessa.

"Of course," Jessa said.

"My lips are sealed," Garrett promised.

After pounding Garrett on the back, Kent turned once more to the house and waddled swiftly toward it. Garrett shook his head, his hands parked at his waist. Finally, he switched his gaze to Jessa.

"I wonder just exactly how he expects to hide something like a swimming pool from Odelia," he said.

Jessa shook her head, smiling wryly. "On the other hand, Kent would do anything for her."

"Obviously." He tilted his head. "They deserve each other, don't you think?"

"I do, yes," Jessa answered.

Garrett's smile softened, his gaze warming, until abruptly he brushed his hands against his thighs. "I'd better get back to work."

"Oh. Okay."

"You guys enjoy yourselves. You picked a good day for it."

"Yes. Thank you."

He stood there a moment longer, almost as if he wanted to say something else, then he turned away. She forbade herself to watch him leave, but his every step brought her a keener sense of loss. She thought of Kent wanting to build a swimming pool for Odelia as a wedding gift, and a yearning that she could not deny rose up in her.

How sweet it would be to trust in love again. But how could she? She was no longer that foolish young girl, but how could she trust her own judgment after Wayne?

Hunter ran up to her, colliding with her knee. "Ready for another load!" he announced happily before dropping to the ground. "Boy, won't Mags be glad for us! Miss Magnolia, I mean. That's what Garrett calls her 'cause he loves her. Mags. But not to her face, for respect."

Jessa bit her lip, suddenly near tears. What sort of man told a child that he loved his elderly benefactress and called her by pet names? "Well, you don't call her Mags to her face, either," she warned gently.

"I know," Hunter replied matter-of-factly. "Garrett says it's respected to call 'em the misses 'cause that's how they were raised."

"It's respectful," Jessa corrected. "And Garrett's right."

"What does that mean?" Hunter asked. "How they were raised?"

"It means how their parents taught them to behave," Jessa told him gently.

"Oh," Hunter said. "Like you teach me."

"Yes."

"And Garrett," he added, busily dumping rose petals into his toy truck. "He teaches me, too. Lots of stuff. Like sashay."

And Garrett, she admitted, if only to herself. *God in Heaven, help me.*

On the other hand, it was time she helped herself instead of sitting around here waiting for the ax to fall. What was she doing, living on charity when she could be working at a job?

Buoyed a little by that thought, Jessa let Hunter play awhile longer, then she settled him in the kitchen with a snack and went to the library to use the phone. Abby readily agreed to drive her down to the employment office the next day and note any possible job openings in the morning paper. Now all that remained was to enlist Carol's help with Hunter. Once she began working, Abby could watch him and help him with his lessons.

Yes, that sounded fine. Jessa reasoned that she could add to her pitiful savings and still handle the wedding flowers. Then, when the inevitable came, she would at least be better prepared to move on, safe if not heart-whole, after all.

The arrival of an automobile at Chatam House did not often snag Garrett's attention, but he happened to be going in for lunch when he first saw the inexpensive little coupe turn off the street. He couldn't help wondering who had come to call, so he bypassed the kitchen in order to glance down the west hallway into the foyer, only to see Jessa sailing out the door. Wearing her best dress slacks and that adorable little ivory blouse with the short, banded sleeves, her long hair rolled up on the back of her head and secured with a large clip, she looked like a lady with a purpose.

Extremely curious now, Garrett backtracked to the kitchen, carrying his empty Thermos. Hilda greeted him with a smile and a ham-and-cheese sandwich.

"Join my other favorite boy at the table," she directed, taking the Thermos from him. "I'll take care of this."

"Garrett's not a boy!" piped a familiar voice.

"He's a boy to me," Hilda insisted, nodding at Garrett.

Grinning, he carried his plate to the table and sat down next to Hunter, foolishly glad to see the kid. Somehow, his days were never quite complete now unless he spent some time with Hunter. He just wished that didn't make Hunter's mother uncomfortable.

"So I'm not a boy, huh?"

"No! Silly. You're all growed up."

Hilda set a tall tumbler of iced tea in front of him, asking, "You want that Thermos filled with a cold drink?"

"Yes, please," Garrett confirmed. "Iced tea, if you have it." She trundled off, nodding. Garrett chomped into his sandwich.

The boy bit off a large chunk of his own sandwich and began to chew industriously. Amused because he knew that he was being copied, Garrett patiently waited for the child to wash down his food with a drink of milk. He lifted his paper napkin and wiped his mouth so Hunter would do the same before asking nonchalantly, "So where's your mom?"

"She went with Abby."

"Ah. They doing anything in particular?"

Hunter shrugged. "The 'ploymint office. It's not fun," he added, "so I should stay here. Mommy said."

She'd decided to find a job, had she? Did that mean she'd given up on opening her shop or was this just another way to avoid him? Despite a sour feeling in his belly, Garrett smiled at Hunter and asked, "So what are you doing today?"

Again, Hunter shrugged. "I dunno. What are *you* doing?"

"I'm mowing," Garrett answered, watching the boy's eyes light up. Like all boys, he was fascinated by vehicles of any sort. "Want to ride along?"

The kid practically came up out of his seat with excitement. "Sure!"

"You have to wear a helmet and protective clothing," Garrett warned, "and before you ask, no, you cannot drive." The tractor had a wide seat and a mowing deck, and it was nearly impossible to turn over, but knowing how protective Jessa could be, Garrett wasn't taking any chances. She wouldn't be pleased as it was, but what could it hurt, really, for the kid to spend a little time with him? Let her grouse. At least she'd be talking to him.

"You can oversee this," Hilda said to Hunter, placing the refilled Thermos on the table.

"Cool!" Hunter decreed.

"I'll let Carol know he'll be spending the afternoon with you," Hilda volunteered, glancing at Garrett.

Nodding his thanks, Garrett finished his lunch, then took Hunter out to the garage and dressed him in an old bicycle helmet and T-shirt. He stepped into a pair of lightweight coveralls to protect his own clothing. They spent the next four hours cutting the grass on the estate, and despite the protective clothing, they were both covered head to toe with dust and grass clippings when they were done, which meant that the kid was going to need a bath before he could put in an appearance at the dinner table. Garrett supposed he was up to overseeing one small boy's bath. After considering all options, Garrett decided to take Hunter up to the suite that he shared with his mother. His clean clothes were there, after all.

As they climbed the stairs, Garrett thoughtlessly patted the curving mahogany banister and admitted, "I always wonder what it would be like to slide down this thing. Don't you?" Hunter gaped at him. "Guess not," Garrett muttered to himself.

He was careful to avoid Jessa's bedroom once they reached the suite, though he stood for several seconds in the sitting room just looking around at her things before following Hunter into his room.

The boy pulled clean clothes from the dresser and turned to face Garrett. "I use the tub in Mommy's room."

Garrett shook his head. He would not trespass on Jessa's personal space. "Not today."

Hunter shrugged and bounced into the bathroom. Garrett followed to set the stopper and start the water in the tub, a deep, old-fashioned claw-foot type, one of the few left in the house. Hunter proclaimed himself able to bathe alone, so Garrett stood outside the bathroom door, listening for sounds of dangerous activity. Finally, he insisted that Hunter get out. Garrett mopped up after him while the boy dressed. Afterward, he looked like a frazzled porcupine.

"Where's your comb?" Garrett asked with a chuckle.

"In Mommy's room."

"Okay. You run and get it."

He followed the boy into the sitting room, but before Hunter returned with the comb, Jessa came in. Sighing, she slung her handbag onto the desk and only then realized that Garrett was present.

"Sorry," he said automatically. "Hunter needed a bath, and since his clothes were in his room, I figured it was best done here."

"Oh, you didn't let him bathe in his bathroom, did you?"

"I cleaned up after. It's perfect, I promise."

Hunter returned then. "Mommy!" He ran to Jessa and

wrapped his arms around her waist. "Garrett let me mow with him. I got to ride on the tractor and pour the tea from the fermus, and I had to wear a helmet and a big T-shirt and everything."

Jessa gave him a tired smile, took the comb and began smoothing his hair. "And then you had a bath, I see."

"Uh-huh. It's a cool tub. The water don't go over the sides."

"Is that right?" She seemed crestfallen and subdued rather than angry as Garrett had expected. He wanted to wrap her in his arms, but of course, he didn't.

"Everything okay?" he asked.

"I suppose. Thanks for putting up with this guy today."

"No problem. You know I enjoy having him around."

She smiled wanly at that. "We'll let you go now," she said, her gaze averted. "I'm sure you have other things to do."

Nodding, Garrett slowly started for the door. She told Hunter that it was time to start his lessons. "Find your copy book."

Hunter ran into his bedroom. She walked around the sofa and plopped down with a sigh. Troubled, Garrett turned back.

"Something wrong?"

Jessa leaned forward, braced her elbows atop her knees and dropped her face into her hands. Alarmed now, Garrett skirted the sofa and dropped down next to her.

"Hey, now. Whatever it is, it'll work out."

"You cannot possibly know that," she told him impatiently.

"Why don't you tell me about it, and we'll see."

Dropping her hands, she sat back. "I went out looking for a job today, if you must know."

"Yeah, Hunter said something about that. I take it things didn't go too well."

"I tried everything I could think of," she reported. "I went to all three florist shops, applied for every job listed with the state employment office, answered every ad. I didn't get a single interview! Do you know that half of the companies have changed their minds? 'We have decided not to fill the position at this time,'" she mimicked. "I heard it a dozen times!"

Garrett reached over and briefly squeezed her hand. "It's not like you really need a job just now," he pointed out.

She shot up to her feet and turned on him. "I can't just sit here day after day, waiting for someone else to decide my future! If I could just earn a little extra cash, I'd feel like I have *some* control!"

An idea struck Garrett, but he didn't dare mention it. Instead, he rose to awkwardly pat her shoulder, and fell back on his previous blandishment. "It'll work out."

Gusting a sigh, she turned and dropped down on the sofa again. "Yeah, yeah, I suppose. I just wish…" She shook her head.

Hunter returned just then with a dog-eared notebook in hand. Jessa forced a smile for him and reached out with one hand, drawing him to her. Garrett laid a hand on the boy's damp head, saying, "Thanks for handling the tea out there today."

"You're welcome."

He left the boy smiling and the mother slumped in what looked very much like defeat, concern clearly writ on her face. Instead of going to the stairs, however, he walked across the landing and down a short hallway to the set of rooms known as the East Suite. Tapping lightly on the door, he waited until finally Kent opened it.

"Can I have a word with you?" Garrett asked, slipping through the door and closing it softly behind him. "I need a favor."

Chapter Ten

Garrett walked into the dining room, his black hair glistening from a recent shower. Jessa watched him move around the table and take a seat next to Hunter before she remembered to drop her gaze. Why was it that she couldn't get out of her head the picture of him standing there in her sitting room, having just overseen her son's bath? And if that weren't bad enough, she'd spilled her guts to him. Again. If only he weren't so easy to talk to. She forced herself to engage with the others at the table, everyone but him.

Even with Ellie and Asher in attendance tonight, the Chatam sisters seemed deeply pleased. After the blessing, Hunter entertained everyone with the story of his mowing adventure. Even Garrett seemed surprised and interested in his descriptions of dirt clods crushed beneath the tractor's wheels and random bird feathers being spewed out by the cutter as tiny bits of fluff.

"And I thought he was just riding along pouring tea," Garrett quipped when Hunter wound down. Everyone laughed, and Garrett began asking everyone about his or her day. He went through all three Chatam sisters and Kent before he got to Jessa.

She'd been trying to decide how she would answer, but

what difference did it make when she'd already told him all about the day's failure? She'd whipped up a good bit of resentment by the time he finally looked past Hunter and asked, "How about you, Jessa? How was your day out with your friend Abby?"

Leaving her fork and knife on her plate, she wiped her hands on the linen napkin and managed an amused tone in her voice. "Well, I think I set a new record for the number of times I've been told no in a single afternoon."

"Oh, my dear!" exclaimed Odelia. "Whoever could refuse you?"

"I suppose it depends on the request," Magnolia reasoned.

"Can we do anything?" Hypatia asked.

Jessa shook her head, blinking against a sudden welling of tears. She didn't know why she felt so keenly disappointed. Perhaps because she'd thought that she and God had made a deal of sorts. A job was to be her consolation prize for ultimately losing the Monroe place.

Garrett cleared his throat and gently said, "Jessa went out looking for a job this afternoon."

To the chorus of protests around the table, she said, "It's still weeks yet before I begin work on the flowers for Ellie's wedding. I can't just sit here day after day doing nothing. I thought a job would fill the gap, and help me save some money for the future. Even a part-time job would've helped, but absolutely no one is hiring."

"Well, if it's a part-time job that you want," Kent said offhandedly, "we have an opening at the pharmacy."

Jessa's mouth dropped open. "What?"

"It's nothing special, of course, and the pay reflects that, I'm afraid." He tapped his chin with the tip of one finger. "Morning hours, which means that most of the fountain drinks will be coffee-based. You'll need to operate a scanner and cash register, but that's no issue, I'm sure. Dusting, stocking…that's about it. The evening workers mop the floors." He looked up, smiling at Jessa. "How does that sound?"

She fought the urge to jump up and kiss him. "That's *fine!* It sounds *fine.*"

"Well, then, you can start tomorrow morning at eight. Unless you'd rather not work on a Saturday."

Jessa laughed. She couldn't help it. "No! That is, I don't mind working on Saturday at all. Thank you."

He shrugged and went back to his meal, but Jessa noticed that she wasn't the only one who looked at him with fond amazement. Odelia's melting smile showered him with adoration, and Garrett was beaming like a lighthouse beacon.

"I told you it would work out."

He *had* told her, but she chose to ignore that little fact for now. "I-I'll arrange for Abby to pick us up at seven-thirty in the morning," she said, planning aloud. "She'll keep Hunter with her and return for me at the end of my shift."

"Oh, there's no need for that," Hypatia said. "There are enough adults in this house to look after one well-behaved little boy."

"And by working part-time, you'll still have time to give him his lessons," Garrett pointed out.

"No school on Saturday," Hunter chimed in, lest anyone get confused and make him do lessons the next day.

Jessa laughed again, her dark mood instantly transformed to delight. "No lessons on Saturday," she confirmed.

"And no reason at all to inconvenience Abby," Magnolia said complacently. "Garrett will see that you get to and from the pharmacy. Won't you, dear?"

Garrett dutifully bobbed his head. "Yes, ma'am. Be happy to."

Jessa smiled, too joyful to worry about the sudden propitious turn of events. "Thank you. Thank you all."

"I feel so happy," Odelia warbled, gazing at Kent. A look passed between them, so ardent that Jessa had to look away.

No man had ever looked at her like that. She felt a stab of envy. Odelia had found love late in her life, but at least she had found it. Maybe, when Jessa was Odelia's age.... Just then, Asher chuckled quietly at something Ellie said, and Jessa's gaze darted across the table. Ellie had laid her hand over his wrist as she leaned in close to speak into his ear, and the light in his eyes burned brightly enough to ignite the tablecloth where he stared at it. Jessa dropped her gaze to her plate.

The world had never seemed so unfair as it did in that moment, or she so alone—until she remembered that she had a job! And friends.

No longer able to deny such an obvious truth, she glanced around the table, taking in every smiling face but one.

"The truck needs gassing up," Garrett said, thrusting the helmet at her. It was the exact truth. The truck did need gas. He saw no point in telling her that it had enough fuel to get her to work and then on to the fueling station.

She took the helmet without a word and released the clip that held her long hair in a clump at her nape. The wheat-brown mass tumbled about her slender shoulders. Garrett had to turn away to keep from reaching out to touch it. When he turned back, she had fixed the helmet in place and the clip had disappeared into a pocket of the blue Monroe Pharmacy smock that she wore over her jeans and T-shirt. Ellie had come up with the smock after dinner last night. Tiny Jessa could have worn it as a dress. Kent, God bless him, had promised to find a smaller one. Meanwhile, she'd make do. Garrett had the feeling that she was very good at making do.

He slung his leg over the bike saddle and waited for Jessa to settle in behind him. Leveling the motorcycle, he put up the kickstand and reached for the ignition. This time, Jessa's arms curled around his waist without any prompting. Garrett smiled to himself. Progress. He hoped.

Less than ten minutes later, he parked the bike at the corner in front of the pharmacy on the downtown square. Garrett walked to the door and found it locked. He tapped and stood back as a man in a lab coat hurried to let them in. The pale eyes behind the round glasses on his round face measured Jessa with bald interest as Garrett introduced Kent's younger partner to their new employee.

"Mildred!" he called over his shoulder before turning back to Jessa with a smile and an explanation. "Millie's been here since the doors opened. She'll be training you."

Millie turned out to be even smaller than Jessa and stooped with age, her back so bent that she could barely look up from the floor, but she waved toward the soda fountain along the inner wall. "We'll start over here. Coffee should be made by now."

"I'd welcome a cup," Garrett said. Jessa pushed her helmet at him before turning to follow the old woman moving at a snail's pace past the aisles of shelves bearing products. Carrying both helmets, Garrett brought up the rear. Kent's partner, a pharmacist like Kent himself, moved toward the prescription counter at the back of the store.

Garrett took a seat on a chrome-and-red vinyl stool at the chrome-and-black counter. Millie pulled a heavy china cup from beneath the counter, placed it in front of him then added a narrow paper napkin and a spoon before listing a number of flavorings available.

"Just plain black coffee, thank you," Garrett told her.

He sipped the dark brew and watched with unabashed fascination as Millie took Jessa through the workings of the old-fashioned soda fountain, recipe by recipe in the book literally chained to the back wall. Millie moved slowly, but she talked fast, and Garrett could see Jessa's eyes glazing over halfway through.

"Just study the recipes and you'll be fine," Millie finished up. "When you're done, you can join me in Cold Medicines, and I'll show you how to read the bar codes."

With that, she turned and shuffled off, presumably to the Cold Medicines aisle. Jessa flipped the recipe book back to the beginning and stood perusing it for several moments. Then she idly turned to lean against the back counter, and the chain affixed to the wall yanked the book right out of her hands. Throwing them up, she moved to leave the fountain area. Garrett quickly pushed his cup to the edge of the counter for a refill.

"If you wouldn't mind...."

She halted to glare at him, then a reluctant smile tugged at her lips. "What are you still doing here anyway?"

"Drinking coffee," he replied as she refilled his cup. Suddenly impatient with this whole situation, he asked, "Why are *you* here?"

She slid the coffee pot back onto the burner. "I need to make some money. Nearly every cent of my savings is tied up in supplies for the flower shop."

"So open the shop," he told her.

She parked her hands at her waist. "And where exactly do you suggest I do that?"

"At the Monroe place, of course."

She dropped her hands, asking avidly, "So you're giving up your claim to it?"

All she wanted was to get rid of him. But all he really wanted was to look after her and Hunter. Just to look after them. Was that too much to ask?

"I'm suggesting that we share it," he told her bluntly. "The more I think about it, the more I'm sure it would work. You and Hunter can move into the house and open your shop. I'll build my nursery in the backyard." She started shaking her head. "I'll stay on at Chatam House and work part-time," he argued. "There's just no reason not to do it."

"I don't see it that way," she said, folding her arms. "It's too…"

"Too what?" he demanded.

"Too risky."

"That's nonsense! The businesses clearly complement each other. You and Hunter will have the house to yourselves. What's risky about that?"

She bit her lip. "I don't know."

"Just think about it," he urged, rising to toss a five-dollar bill onto the counter. "See you at one."

"Oh, no," she said quickly. "Abby offered to give me a lift home when I called her to tell her about the job last night."

Disappointed, he snapped, "Fine! Just don't forget that we have a meeting to plan the wedding reception. And keep the change."

Grabbing up both helmets, he strode out of there before he said or did something that he'd regret. Like kiss her. That's what he wanted to do, he realized, just grab her and plant one on her, make her see him as something more than the Chatams' gardener. As he strapped down the extra helmet on the back of the bike, he admitted to himself that it wouldn't work between them. There were things about him that she didn't know, things that would make her even more wary than she was now. He'd tried to tell her the other day at the rose arbor, but he couldn't bear to see the disgust on her face.

What difference did it make, anyway? She'd made her lack of personal interest perfectly clear. She was not for him. Period. Might as well accept that fact.

Still, he was right about sharing the Monroe Place. It made perfect sense. The businesses did complement each other, and the space was large enough for both. She and Hunter would have a home of their own, and he would be able to see them, watch over them. Until some other guy came along and snapped her up.

Depressed, he spent the morning in a pall, doing laundry and straightening his room before going out to gas up the truck and grab a bite of lunch that Hilda would not have to prepare. When he wandered into the ballroom at the appointed time, only Magnolia had arrived before him, and he knew before he'd crossed even half of the expansive room that she'd planned it this way.

"Where is everyone?"

"They'll be along. I wanted a private moment with you. Were you able to speak to Jessa this morning?"

"Sure. When I dropped her off at the pharmacy I went inside and had a cup of coffee."

"And?"

"And nothing."

Mags made an exasperated sound. "Did you suggest that you share the Monroe property?"

"Yes. And she refused."

"Why?"

"Too 'risky.'" He lifted both forefingers and curled them to indicate quotation marks.

"Utter nonsense," Magnolia grumbled. "It's the perfect solution."

"I know that."

Magnolia tapped the cleft in her chin with a forefinger. "Someone has to convince her."

"Don't look at me," he said. "I've tried."

"Try harder. It's the only fair thing for both of you." He didn't care about fair anymore; he only cared about Jessa and Hunter, but he didn't tell Mags that. She smiled and said, "I'll say a prayer for you."

"Better be that praying without ceasing thing," he grumbled, and she laughed.

Ellie waltzed into the room just then, followed by Asher, Hypatia, Odelia, Kent, Hilda and Chester. He glanced at his watch and wondered when Jessa would arrive. She should've left work ten minutes ago. Corralling his thoughts onto the subject at hand, he listened as Ellie chattered about the wedding, but in the back of his mind ran Magnolia's words.

So convince her. Try harder. It's the perfect solution. I'll say a prayer.

He sent up his own prayer, because the sooner he could convince her, the better for everyone.

"Thanks, Abby." Releasing her seat belt, Jessa leaned across the little car and hugged her mother's old friend before hopping out to run up the steps and walk through the front door of Chatam House. Knowing that she was expected in the ballroom, she fought the impulse to look for her son and instead journeyed down the right hallway to the double doors that now stood wide open. Everyone turned to look at her the instant that she stepped onto the marble floor of the magnificent room.

Muttering, "Sorry I'm late," she hurried to join the group in the center of the space.

"What do you think?" Ellie asked, bouncing on her toes. "At which end of the room should the bridal party's table be?"

Jessa glanced around. "Neither. I'd put the bridal party at a long table there between the two sets of doors. The gift table could go right across from it." She looked up at the chandelier overhead, adding, "And the cake should go on a round table right here in the center of the floor, with buffet tables coming off it."

Ellie clapped her hands. "Perfect!

"We have four large matching urns," Magnolia said.

"They'll need very large arrangements to balance them, but don't you think that would be enough, even for so large a space?"

Jessa nodded, mentally placing the urns for maximum effect. "We could float violets and candles in bowls of water on the guest tables and string small white lights over the tops of the windows like twinkling valances."

"We have lights like that!" Odelia said excitedly. "Oh, how pretty!"

"We could bring in the topiaries and light those, too," Garrett put in.

Ellie sighed. "It's going to be *so* beautiful."

"Mommy!" Jessa turned toward the sound of her son's voice. He stood with Carol in the open doorway to the hall, gaping at the massive room. Jessa smiled, and he ran forward, crying, "Watch!"

Suddenly, he dropped onto his knees and slid halfway across the room, nearly bowling into the group gathered there. Bodies hopped every which way to avoid a collision. Jessa's jaw dropped, and embarrassment flushed her cheeks with hot color even as the other adults laughed or hid smiles. Hunter had never before done such a thing! Garrett bent and lifted the boy to his feet, then slapped hands with him.

"Good slide!"

"That's more fun than sliding down the banister!" Hunter declared.

Sliding down the banister? Anger boiled up in Jessa. She knew exactly who to blame for this. The guilty glance that Garrett shot in her direction confirmed her worst suspicions. Impulsively, she marched forward and stabbed him in the chest with a forefinger.

"I want a word with you. In private."

Garrett looked around, nodded just once and took her arm. "This way," he said grimly.

He walked her across the floor, out of the room and down the hall to the sunroom, then into the back hallway past the kitchen to the room that they called the family parlor. He shoved the door closed behind them. She rubbed the tingling skin of her arm where he had held it, though he had in no way injured her, and put on her sternest face. She knew that her anger was unreasonable, but nothing had gone as she'd hoped since she'd come to Buffalo Creek, absolutely nothing. And it was all his fault!

"How dare you teach my son such risky behaviors!"

"I didn't."

"Then where did he get such ideas?"

"The same place all kids get them."

"He's never done such things before!" she pointed out hotly.

"He's never been a normal kid before!" Garrett shot back.

Jessa gasped. "There's nothing wrong with my son! He's a quiet, well-behaved little boy, and you have no right—"

"None at all," Garrett agreed, interrupting. "But that's not going to stop me. Not any longer."

She opened her mouth to respond, but his big hands reached for her and dragged her against him. The next thing she knew, he was kissing her.

Stunned, Jessa froze. And then she melted. She couldn't help it. She had no defenses against such sweet heat or the joy that burst within her as Garrett's arms gently closed around her, tucking her against his chest, her head nesting in the hollow of his shoulder, her face turned up to his. She knew she had only to step away to put a stop to this, but that single step seemed beyond her. The anger dissipated like steam released into the air, and she knew that on some level she had been waiting, hoping for this.

"Ah, Jess," he whispered against her lips. "Jessa."

And then he kissed her again. Or did she kiss him this

time? She feared it was the latter, but she couldn't seem to stop. Finally, he did.

"I've wanted to do that for a long time," he admitted, making her smile.

"Have you? I—I wasn't sure."

He cupped her cheek in the palm of his hand. "I half expected you to slap me," he told her wryly.

"I should," she muttered. "I think. I don't know. There's just too much to consider."

He pushed out a gusty sigh and tilted back his head. "You're right. Okay. Put the two of us aside for a moment. We'll take this step by step." Drawing her over to the sofa, he sat down there with her, both of her hands in his.

"Let's start with Hunter. He's blossoming. Don't you see that? He's no longer cowering in fear and protecting himself in silence. He's stepping out of his shell, daring to try new things. That's all that was back there. As for my influencing him, I may have *mentioned* sliding down the banister to him, but I didn't do it with him or show him how, and I was as surprised by that grand slide across the ballroom floor as you were. But it's no big deal. I'll make sure he knows that he shouldn't do it again, if only because he'll tear the knees out of his pants. Okay?"

She managed a nod, fresh color rising to her face now that she could think of her anger and the kiss—kisses—sanely.

"You shouldn't cower in fear any longer, either," he told her, smoothing her hair with one hand.

She realized that it had fallen and reached back to pluck out the clip. "I'm not."

"You are," he argued. "And I don't blame you. But, honey, you've never been safer than you are right now. Please, please, understand that."

Tears filled her eyes, but she managed to ignore the endearment and squeak, "I do. Really, I do."

He sighed with relief. "Good. Then you'll think about the two of us sharing the Monroe place, won't you? I mean really, seriously think about it. I'm convinced that both of our businesses would benefit if we share the space."

She nodded. In truth, she couldn't help thinking about it. She'd thought about it all day even though she'd tried not to. He clasped her hands again.

"You could set up shop in the back parlor rather than the front," he said eagerly. "I'll build the nursery between the garage and the shed. We could gravel the space between your shop and the nursery for parking. That way the front door is yours, and you could use the butler's pantry as workspace."

He was right. That would be perfect, far better than using the front room for her shop, but she just couldn't tell him yes. She had to think this through carefully.

"Tell you what," Garrett said squeezing her hands. "Let's pray about it. Right now. Together."

Jessa looked up at him in wonder. He wanted to pray with her? Now?

Wayne had only ever prayed in church. Now that she thought about it, she realized that she had only ever seen him pray when others could also see him doing so. But here sat Garrett Willows, urging her to private prayer. Jessa nodded.

Garrett closed his eyes and bowed his head, bringing his brow to hers. "Lord, thank You for bringing Jessa and Hunter here. Please keep them safe. You know our needs and dreams. You know what is best for us. If sharing the Monroe property is not best for all for us, then please show us that. And if it is the best thing, help us see that, too. That's all either of us want, Lord, the best for everyone involved. So, we're asking You, in the name of Christ Jesus, to guide us. Amen."

"Amen," Jessa whispered.

Garrett kissed her forehead, slipped an arm around her

shoulders and leaned back against the flowered, overstuffed cushions with her. "Think it over," he said. "You don't have to decide today. As for us," he went on softly, "I don't want you to worry about what just happened. We'll take it slow, just see where things go between us. I'll give you all the room and time you need, I promise. And if things don't go anywhere, that's okay. But I hope you know how much I've come to care about you. I think I have from the beginning, really, from the moment you tumbled off that ladder into my arms." He chuckled. Then he sobered, promising, "I'll never intentionally do anything to hurt you or Hunter, as God is my witness. Where this goes, what happens between us, that's up to you. Completely. Okay?"

Her mind whirled with all he'd said. It was almost too much to take in. What if he turned out to be just like Wayne? What if her business succeeded and his didn't, or vice versa? She needed time to think it through, bit by bit. And wasn't that exactly what he was offering her?

Blinking back grateful tears, she nodded and whispered, "Okay."

Smiling, he sighed again and smoothed a hand over her upper arm. "It's all going to work out now. You'll see. Everything's going to be just fine."

She almost believed it. Almost.

Chapter Eleven

❧

"We'd be sharing the utilities as well as the rent," Garrett said softly the next morning, opening the front passenger door of the town car for her. "Consider that. And I've already budgeted the cost of creating the parking space, so don't worry, that's on me."

Jessa laughed as he handed her down into the seat of the car. His enthusiasm seemed to know no bounds, and since their "discussion" in the family parlor the day before, he'd taken every opportunity to sell her on the idea of sharing the Monroe place. Having thought about it—as well as those kisses—all night long, she had to admit that the notion was rapidly growing on her, but she had to be sure. She'd stumbled blindly into marriage and lived to regret it. She couldn't make that kind of mistake again.

Garrett closed the door and hurried around to get in behind the steering wheel. He let the ladies, Kent and Hunter out in front of the church a few minutes later then left to park the car across the square in front of the pharmacy. Jessa wouldn't see him again until they met for worship in the sanctuary just over an hour later.

As before, during corporate prayer, she spoke silently to God, requesting His guidance and wisdom. She knew that

Garrett sat beside her doing the same thing. Perhaps he was even asking God to convince her of the rightness of his plan. Perhaps he even asked for more.

It was the *more* that truly troubled her. Could Garrett actually love her? He hadn't said as much, and she wasn't sure that she wanted him to. At the same time, she wanted it more than anything else, and such neediness frightened her. Was it so wrong, though, to want to be loved?

She didn't doubt that she could love him. In truth, she feared that she already did, but to acknowledge such a thing, even to herself…

Then there was her son to consider. She'd never seen Hunter so happy, so free. He adored Garrett, and Garrett seemed to enjoy him as much as she did. Wayne considered the boy almost a possession, something that she had stolen from him. She wasn't sure that he saw their son as a person at all, only a thing to control, to have. Was it any surprise that Hunter couldn't be his own person around his father? But he could with Garrett. Somehow, Garrett had done what even she could not: he had freed Hunter to be his own person. But what happened if Garrett left them one day or lost his temper and struck out or…

She shook her head. She could invent what if's all day long, but that didn't change the fact she wanted to be free of the fear that had paralyzed her for so long. Free to love.

Did she have the courage for that? She didn't know. She just didn't know. So, she did the only thing that she could think of to do—she told Garrett about her concerns after lunch. It occurred to her, even as they swayed back and forth, side by side, on the swing, that she'd never have done this sort of thing with Wayne.

"I'm not sure I can do it," she admitted to Garrett.

"You can," he told her. "You have more strength than you

know. You had the strength to get out of your situation, and that's so much more than many can say."

"You have to understand. All the years of my marriage, all I ever wanted was to be on my own, to be apart from him."

"From *him*," Garrett echoed. "Not from the world, not from everyone. You just wanted away from the pain and fear. But what about love and support and sharing? No one truly wants to be apart from those things, and those things can only be given to us by others."

He was right. She knew he was right, but could it be so simple as this, so simple as saying yes?

She laid her head on his shoulder. "I don't know."

"Then we'll wait until you do," he said, wrapping his arm around her.

It was the best thing he could have said.

"It's a lot to take in," she told Garrett on Monday. "Because it's not just a business plan."

"It isn't," he admitted, strolling beside her as they walked the perimeter of the estate. He did this a couple times a week, just to be sure that nothing on the fifteen acres needed his attention, and he'd been pleased when Jessa had agreed to walk with him today. Hunter ran ahead, stuffing his pockets with acorns and rocks and oddly shaped twigs. "I could tell you that it is just business," Garrett said, "but it wouldn't be true. I want a life with you and Hunter. I think I have from the beginning, and I think God means it to happen and that's why He brought us together at the Monroe place and now here at Chatam House."

"I thought that way once," she confessed softly, staring off into the distance, "that everything happened for a reason."

Garrett swallowed a lump that had risen in his throat and waited for her to tell him more. There were things that he should tell her, too, but not now. Not yet. They hadn't mattered before, but now they might.

"Wayne was a reporter for a state magazine," she said with a wry smile. "It seemed so glamorous, but the money wasn't very good, and he'd finally worked his way into a management position with stable hours and no travel. He could think about starting a family, he said, and there I was, so young and stupid and so in awe of this older man. I asked myself why he would want me, but it didn't occur to me that it was precisely because I was young and stupid and so in awe of him." She shook her head.

"You aren't quite so young now," Garrett pointed out, "and you're certainly not stupid, and I'm the one in awe of you, I'm afraid."

She laughed at that. Hunter lifted his head from studying something on the ground and came running back to them to see what was so funny. She hadn't told him about the plan, Garrett knew, so he wouldn't. That was her choice to make, her call.

"How old are you anyway?" she asked Garrett suddenly, sliding an arm around Hunter's shoulders.

"I turned twenty-nine on the tenth of April," he told her. "It was the day that Magnolia told me she'd persuaded Kent to seek a combined use zoning for the place on Charter Street."

"Ah. It was meant to be your birthday gift, I see."

"I suspect so. What about you?"

"A woman never tells her true age." It was the first time she'd bantered with him.

"Age and birth date, I'll have them both, thank you," he teased, snapping his finger. "Come on. Give."

"Twenty-six," Hunter supplied.

"Traitor!" she quipped, tapping the end of his nose with her forefinger as they ambled along. "I'll have you know that I'll be twenty-seven on July sixth. And you," she said to Hunter, ruffling his hair, "will be seven on August eighth." She stopped and stared at him. "Goodness me, how can it be?"

Hunter hunched his shoulders. Curly, Kent's old yellow cat, darted out of the shrubbery just then. "There you are!" Hunter called, racing off after the creature. To Garrett's surprise, the tomcat flopped down in a patch of sunshine and let the boy catch up. Hunter fell to his knees and began to pet the mangled yellow fur.

"Seven years old," Jessa said wistfully. "My baby will soon be seven years old."

"Did you never want another child?" Garrett asked gently.

"Not with Wayne," she answered forthrightly, "and he didn't want another, either, thankfully."

"I do," Garrett told her bluntly. "I never thought about it until just now, but I'd love to have a couple more kids."

A couple *more.* As if Hunter were already his to claim. He watched the boy stroke the old yellow cat, and held his breath. She said nothing, just stood there. Then she slipped her hand into his. And squeezed.

He could breathe again.

Jessa lay awake on Tuesday night, thinking. Garrett had presented her with a formal business plan that evening. He would absorb the building costs, but then most of the building was on his end. They were to split the monthly bills evenly, including rent and utilities. The lease would be in her name, so if sharing the place didn't work out, it would revert to her. The generosity of that astounded her. Garrett astounded her.

He'd even figured in the cost of signs and proposed that they dub the site Willow Tree Place. He would call his business Willow Tree Nursery. She liked the sound of Willow

Tree Floral for her shop. Still, she hesitated, and she wasn't really sure why.

Earlier, sitting on the workbench in the greenhouse next to her, Garrett had told her again to take her time. "I'm not trying to rush you," he'd said. "I just thought you should know what I'm thinking."

Feeling his solid warmth along her side from her shoulder to her knee, she'd thumbed through the printed matter he'd given her and listened to his explanations of the charts and columns. It was a good business plan. Garrett had even come up with a used walk-in refrigerator that she could afford, and he denied that either he or the Chatams were footing any part of the cost. He'd thought of things she hadn't, like taking on part-time help and what sort of revenue stream would be needed to pay for it. The amount seemed daunting, but that was not what held her back. She knew in her bones that the shop would be profitable.

She didn't fear the future, either. When she thought about it, when she envisioned what Willow Tree Place might look and feel like, she felt only excitement and hope. More convinced than ever that the Charter Street site was perfect for her, *their,* purposes, she was already mentally stocking the shelves and designing the displays. And Garrett was always right there beside her while she was doing it. She could no longer quite see a future for her and Hunter without Garrett.

So why didn't she say yes? She closed her eyes and imagined Garrett there with her.

"Take all the time you need," he would whisper. *"It's all up to you. I want you to be sure. I want you to be happy with what we're doing."*

She smiled into the night, hunching her shoulders to keep the imagined words close, words he'd already said in one way or another. Suddenly she knew why she continued to delay, and the truth stunned her.

She was enjoying herself!

This was no longer about doubt and fear. This was about those soft, sweet words, about the little touches, the warmth in his sky-blue eyes. This was about being courted, and he was courting her, without doubt.

Wayne had courted her, too. He had, in fact, quite swept her off her feet with calculated looks and touches, and half compliments.

"You would look so beautiful in green," he had said. She had heard "beautiful" and dashed out to buy a green blouse, which he hadn't liked because the stitching was "coarse." She had bought another, one he had picked out.

"You would be smart to accept the guidance of an older individual," he'd told her, meaning himself, of course. She certainly hadn't been smart enough to see through his manipulations. He'd even implied that she was a burden to her mother.

Unlike Wayne, Garrett gave her options. He saw needs that she did not always see herself, even where her son was concerned, but he did not dictate. Garrett offered choices and calm support. Wayne had given, bestowed, as befitted a superior being. Garrett shared. And she loved him for it.

She didn't want to. She didn't *want* to love him and risk her heart. But she wanted to *be* loved. She wanted Garrett to love her. And Hunter.

As selfish as it seemed, she was going to give herself a chance at that love.

She finally agreed to share the Monroe place with him on Wednesday after the midweek prayer service.

"It's really the only fair way," she said.

"Thank you," Garrett told her, closing his eyes and wrapping his arms around her. "Thank you, thank you, thank you." His relief made him light-headed, so he opened his eyes again, gazing out across the moonlight-silvered grass. They stood in the shadow of the massive magnolia tree on the west lawn, chest to chest, their hearts beating in unison.

"If Hunter and I are going to live in the house, though, we should pay more," she insisted.

He shook his head. "I'm content with fifty percent. Why complicate things?"

"I still don't know about *us*," she said into the hollow of his shoulder. "I want that whole happily-ever-after thing, but is that even real?"

"Yes," he said firmly, tightening his embrace, "and I want to give you that. I want to give you that more than anything else in this world."

"I'm not sure this part of it is fair," she admitted. "I'm not sure that you don't feel more for me than I can dare to feel for you."

"You'll learn to trust me," he promised her, "to trust yourself, to trust us, and when you do, you can dare anything."

"I hope so," she whispered.

"I know so," he told her boldly, daring to believe it. And once she did trust him, *them,* he would tell her all. Then he would ask her to marry him—and be prepared for a long engagement. She was understandably skittish, and he didn't deserve her, of course, but he wasn't going to let that stop him, not if God was good enough to give her to him. He smiled to himself and held her tight.

"When do you think we should tell everyone else?" she asked, easing away a little. He loosened his hold. If she wanted space, he would give her space. Whatever she wanted, whatever she needed, he would see that she had it.

"Tomorrow at dinner? That'll give us time to make some plans and iron out as many wrinkles as possible. For instance, would it be best if I put the utilities in my name?"

Jessa considered and decided, "It might make it more difficult for Wayne to track me down. Leases are private. Utilities are part of the public record."

"Then we'll put the utilities in my name."

She smiled and turned up her face. "You know, this could work out very well indeed."

He cupped her lovely face in his hands, promising, "This is all going to work out great. You'll see."

Then he kissed her, and she slipped her arms about his neck and kissed him back.

This was all going to work out wonderfully well, he told himself a little desperately.

Please, God, let it all work out just half as well as I imagine!

Uncertainty swamped Jessa as she faced the dinner table, Garrett at her side, on Thursday evening. They'd purposefully delayed their entrance until everyone else had settled into place. She'd even sent Hunter on ahead to take his seat. Now, she wished that he was there beside her to hold her hand.

She knew that sharing the Monroe place was the right thing, but now that the moment had come to publicly commit herself to Garrett's plan, she could barely breathe for the pounding of her heart.

Father God, don't let me panic now. I know it's best. I know it. But...can I really do this?

Apparently, she could. When Garrett gripped her hand and cleared his throat, calling attention to the two of them, she took a deep breath and felt instantly calmer.

Everyone applauded when Garrett made the announcement, even Hunter, who had no real notion of what was happening.

"Well, it's the perfect solution," Asher said.

"An excellent compromise," Hypatia decreed.

"Sounds as if you have things well in hand," Kent said, giving tacit approval.

"Very well in hand," Magnolia commented pointedly, smiling like a cat at the cream bowl.

"So when is the grand opening?" Odelia wanted to know.

Garrett glanced at Jessa. "We're hoping for a week from this coming Friday," he said. "If ya'll don't mind lending us Dale."

"We can manage that, can't we, my love?" Kent said, looking to Odelia.

"Of course, Mr. Bowen must stop his work here to help you two prepare for your grand openings," Odelia announced magnanimously. "We have time yet to complete our quarters."

"That's very generous," Garrett said. "Thank you."

Jessa quickly addressed Ellie. "I know this plan gives me less than a week to do the flowers for your wedding, but I'll have them ready, I promise." She turned her gaze to Kent next. "And I won't let you down at the pharmacy, either. I'll stay on until you find a replacement."

"Oh, my dear," Kent chuckled, "don't concern yourself. We never had an opening in the first place. I offered the job merely because Garrett thought it would make you feel better."

Jessa gasped. "You gave me a job when you didn't need the help?"

Odelia laid her head on his shoulder, crooning, "Isn't he wonderful?"

"Oh, my goodness!" Jessa clapped a hand over her mouth, tears filling her eyes.

She glanced around the table and took in the slightly apologetic expressions. Had everyone known? Everyone but her? She couldn't help feeling a little foolish—until her gaze settled finally on the man at her side. Then she simply felt blessed. She had never known such kindness as she'd found here, such thoughtfulness.

Garrett slipped a comforting arm about her shoulders, and Hunter smiled, his lips curved in a perfect crescent. Dashing away tears with one hand, Jessa burbled with laughter. "You're all such dear, caring people. I don't know how I'll ever repay your generosity."

"But don't you see?" Hypatia said. "We have our own personal florist now!"

"Indeed, you do," Jessa agreed, laughing. "You'll never be turned away from my shop."

"Well, then, I'd say it's worth it," Magnolia put in, smiling at Garrett. "Very much so."

"Oooh," Odelia cooed, "we have to come up with the perfect grand-opening gifts."

"Now, don't go overboard," Garrett cautioned sternly, but then a smile broke out across his face.

They were all smiling. Especially Jessa. Yes, doubts remained, but she truly believed she was doing the right thing. As scary as it was to trust again, she just couldn't convince herself that Garrett was anything other than the wonderful man he seemed or that the future could be anything other than bright.

Time did not just fly; it swirled, dipped, spiraled, dived and at times came to a screeching halt. They had a brief tiff with the Historical Society when several of its members took umbrage at the heavy glass door that Jessa bought to replace the paneled back door at the Monroe house. Magnolia managed to smooth that over by having Garrett install the glass door over the original, which could be pushed back against the wall during business hours. Dozens of other mini crises cropped up on a daily basis and were somehow overcome, until only the final details remained.

Dizzied by a week and a half of activity and decisions, Jessa could hardly credit that the day of the "Great Grand Opening," as the Chatams called it, would arrive with the morning. Meanwhile, one last glass shelf remained to be bolted into place. She steadied the brass bracket while Garrett made short work of driving the screw into the wall and reached for another. Hunter ran into the room through the open door to the hallway.

"Look who I found!"

Garrett glanced around, grinning at the cat that Hunter clutched against his chest. "Looks like Curly has come home."

"Can we keep him?" Hunter begged. "Pleeease?"

Jessa shook her head at the scraggly animal. Its mottled yellow fur bore the dark scars of the fire that had closed the Monroe house a few months earlier. Garrett had told her that the cat—along with Asher's sister, Dallas—had caused the fire by knocking over a can of paint remover and a burning lamp. Dallas had reportedly loosened the cap on the paint remover in an effort to fill the house with fumes and drive the Monroes out, intending to see them sheltered at Chatam House in an attempt to reunite Kent and Odelia. The fire had been unplanned, but her scheme had worked. The cat, however, remained a free spirit.

"He's a free-roaming tom, son. I'm not sure anyone can 'keep' him."

"I expect he'll be around quite a lot, though," Garrett commented. "Kent won't mind sharing him."

"Cool," Hunter said. "He can sleep on my bed." With that, he turned and ran from the room with the cat.

Jessa huffed unhappily, but Garrett quickly sought to soothe her. "Don't worry. Even if Hunter can keep the cat in tonight, old Curly isn't likely to hang around for long. He'll be out of here as soon as the door is opened in the morning, I guarantee."

Giving him a doubtful look, Jessa subsided and went to fetch the glass for the shelf. She smiled to herself as he set the rest of the screws. He was always doing that, easing her concerns. He'd met every problem with calm reason and hard work, coming up with creative solutions and implementing them swiftly. She'd come to depend on him completely. And, yes, to trust him.

She passed him the glass panel, and he fit it securely into the brackets. Finished with the task at hand, he paused to look around them.

"Sweetheart, I think that's it."

Warmth swept through her at the endearment, but she refused to wallow in it.

"Not quite," she refuted. "I have to decorate these shelves yet."

"That's your department," he told her, starting to put away his tools.

He carried the toolbox outside while she rushed into the workroom to begin gathering up the things that she'd set out to display. Garrett came in again and helped her carry stuff into the outer room, but then Hunter reappeared, declaring that he was starving. He seemed to be eating the equivalent of his own weight every day right now. Perhaps because he'd run so free these past weeks.

"I'll make him a sandwich," Garrett said, waving her back to the job.

"Thank you."

"No problem. It's dinnertime, you know."

Jessa shook her head. She hadn't even noticed. Garrett left the room. She stepped back to view her handiwork sometime later and heard him tell Hunter that he needed a bath before bed.

"O-kay," Hunter acquiesced reluctantly. Then they both trooped up the stairs. A few moments later, she heard the sound of water running overhead.

Jessa's heart swelled. How many times over the past ten or eleven days had Garrett stepped in to take care of her son when it was more convenient for him than her? He had fit himself seamlessly into the lives they were building here. She loved it all, this house, the shop, the way Hunter had blossomed and grown, how easily Garrett dealt with him. Garrett himself. It was all perfect. He was perfect, everything she'd ever dreamed of in a man.

She suspected that he would ask her to marry him before too long, and she wondered if she would agree. In truth, she'd prefer not to marry again, but she couldn't deny that she loved Garrett and didn't want to lose him. And then there were those "couple more" kids, he'd mentioned. She knew that if she wanted a rich, full life with him, all she had to do was reach out and take it. If she had the courage. She hoped she would, for all their sakes.

Chapter Twelve

The display done, Jessa went upstairs to look in on Hunter and Garrett. She heard Hunter's laughter long before she reached the upper hall.

Garrett leaned a shoulder against the doorjamb and stared into the bedroom across from the bath, allowing Hunter the privacy he now demanded. "No, I'm serious," he said. "Hamsters will eat right through your wall. They'll eat your plumbing if it's that plastic pipe. They're just big rats, after all. You're better off with a dog. Once Curly shows it who's boss, they'll get along just fine."

"You think Curly can beat up a dog?" Hunter asked from the tub.

"Yeah, most of them. Any dog your mom would let you have, anyway."

Jessa slipped into Hunter's room and quietly laid out his pajamas. A dog, was it? They'd have to see about that. Oh, who was she kidding? They'd get a dog if that was what Hunter wanted, something small and easily housebroken. Something Curly would no doubt put in its place and Garrett would patiently train. Jessa smiled to herself. A cat, a dog, a couple more kids and Garrett. Could life get any better than that?

Hunter ran into the room a few moments later, trailing water and flapping towels. Garrett gathered the towels as they were discarded and began mopping up the water while Hunter got into his pj's.

"Can I watch TV, Mom?"

He'd started calling her "Mom" instead of "Mommy" lately. She took it as a bittersweet sign that he was growing up.

"Half an hour," she told him, and he scampered into the upstairs sitting room that they'd created in the large bedroom overlooking the front of the house. She went to turn on the television and thought she heard a knock downstairs.

"I'll check," Garrett volunteered.

He returned just in time to help tuck in Hunter and got a hug for his efforts.

"Sleep well, buddy. Big day tomorrow."

To Jessa's surprise—and apparently Garrett's, too—Curly jumped up onto the bed and plopped down next to Hunter. They left him talking to the mangy old cat.

"I bet you could beat up even a big dog, but I'll look for a friendly one so you don't have to."

Jessa and Garrett kept their laughter to themselves as they moved away.

"What took so long?" Jessa asked as Garrett steered her down the stairs. "You were gone quite a while."

"I'll show you," he answered, escorting her to the dining room.

He'd laid out a candlelit dinner. She recognized the plates from Chatam House.

"Hilda indulged me. I thought we deserved a special celebration after all our hard work."

Jessa laughed, surprised by the huskiness of her own voice. "It's lovely."

He seated her at the head of the ornate dining table, which

belonged to the Monroes and had escaped the fire, before taking the place to her right. After pouring them large goblets of Hilda's special lemonade, he lifted his glass in a toast.

"To the grandest of openings."

"The grandest of openings," she repeated, clinking her glass against his.

"And to us," he added softly.

"And to us," she echoed in a whisper, taking a sip.

Grinning, he took a long slug of the sweet lemonade, and Jessa laughed again. She'd been doing that a lot lately, laughing. By the time dinner was finished—a lovely crab-filled chicken breast, angel-hair pasta and Hilda's fabulous apple walnut salad—she wondered if she had ever laughed so much in her life.

As they washed the dishes and packed up the detritus of their meal for the return trip to Chatam House, her heart began to beat in a slow, steadily more pronounced cadence, for she knew what was coming next. Wayne had been stinting with his affection, withholding it as punishment when displeased; not so with Garrett, though he never pressed her, never demanded.

Leaning a hip against the counter, he slowly pulled her to him and pressed his lips to hers. Lifting his head a long while later, he smiled.

"See you in the morning, partner."

"I'll have the coffee ready," she promised, and he went out smiling.

She couldn't help loving him. Hugging herself, she wondered how long before she completely lost herself to him? Or was it too late already? And would that really turn out to be so bad, after all?

"Of course, she's fallen in love with him," Magnolia said from the end of the couch in the private sitting room that she shared with her sisters. "What young woman in her right mind wouldn't fall in love with Garrett? Especially given how much time they've spent together lately."

Odelia shrugged, tucking her feet beneath her.

"They have spent a lot of time together," Hypatia said, lowering herself into the armchair opposite the sofa with a sigh, "but you must admit, dear, that not every young woman would overlook Garrett's unfortunate past."

Magnolia mentally scoffed at Hypatia's concern. Anyone with any sense would understand completely. Still, a tiny, niggling doubt wormed its way in, nonetheless.

"You don't think she would reject him because of it, do you?"

"I don't know, dear," Hypatia answered. "What did Garrett say about it?"

What had Garrett said about it? Magnolia wondered. Goodness, did Jessa even *know?*

A terrible urgency seized her. "I have to speak to someone," she said, rising to her feet. "If I don't see you later, good night, girls."

"Good night," Hypatia said.

"Good night!" Odelia called gaily. "I feel like a girl, you know," she said with a giggle. "That's what love does for you."

Magnolia would take her word for it and pray that it also did much, much more.

Humming to himself, Garrett drove the old truck toward Chatam House. The spring night sent warm air rushing across the forearm that he rested along the edge of the open window. The sensation made him think of Jessa. He chuckled aloud.

What didn't make him think of Jessa?

He was obsessed with the woman and happily so. The

truth was, he loved her, and her son, so much that it shocked him. It even frightened him a little.

Almost since he'd met her, Garrett had walked on eggshells around Jessa for fear that he'd frighten or offend her, but lately…lately he'd begun to relax. He couldn't seem to help himself. Being with her felt like the most natural thing in the world.

That shouldn't be so surprising, really. Jessa and he had much in common, more than he'd even realized. Yes, they both had experience with abusive situations. Over these past days, however, he'd come to see that it was more than that. They worked together with the ease of long-time partners, and they often reached the same decision independently. Their personal tastes dovetailed neatly, too.

Once, he'd paused in the yard on his way to the house, caught by the mellow sunshine and velvet air, only to rouse himself and go inside to find Jessa basking in the open window, eyes closed, inhaling gently as the Texas spring enveloped her. He'd wanted to fall at her feet and tell her then how he felt, but he'd held his tongue. He'd promised her time, after all.

Later, after a long, busy day, Garrett had offered to buy dinner. Hunter immediately called for pizza, but Garrett and Jessa had looked at each other and said, "Tacos!" It turned out that they liked the same kind from the same place.

Smiling at the memory, Garrett slowed the truck at the entrance to the estate and turned off the street into the drive, moving slowly and carefully past the open, black wrought-iron gate with the stylized gold C at the center top. Oh, how he would miss this place and everyone in it when the day came to finally leave! But he trusted that he would be going to something even better, his own home. Perhaps even to his own wife and family. Yes, it had gotten that serious for him.

Garrett sensed that Jessa was coming around to the possibility of a future with him, but he well knew that she was in no hurry to truly consider such a thing. He sensed as well that, if he was not careful, he could find himself permanently trapped in a kind of limbo with her, forever on the periphery of her life, never truly held in her heart. He prayed for God's guidance and timing. He didn't want to press her, but he didn't want to wait too long for a decision from her, either.

After guiding the old truck through the porte cochere at the west end of the house, he parked it in the garage and ascended the stairs to the living quarters above. He let himself into the narrow front hall and went straight to the attic steps, only to halt at the sound of Magnolia's voice.

"Garrett."

Turning, he saw her standing in the doorway of the living room, backlit by Chester's television set.

"Mags? Uh, Magnolia." Given the hour, he couldn't help a spurt of alarm. "Is everything okay?"

"I just wanted a moment to talk to you. We've hardly seen you these past couple of weeks."

He relaxed a bit. "I know. I'm sorry. I'll make up the time. There's just been so much to do."

"This isn't about that. It's another matter. May I come up?"

Surprised by this, he glanced up the narrow stairs. "Are you sure?"

"Please."

"O-of course."

Confused and curious, he stepped away from the foot of the stairs and lifted an arm in invitation. Magnolia moved forward and began the climb. He came after her, wondering what could be so important that she would come here and seek him out.

The door to his room stood open as usual, and she walked in without hesitation, glancing around at the spartan décor. He preferred it that way, from the simple quilt on his narrow bed to the faded armchair positioned beside the window. She went there and sat on the edge of the seat cushion. Garrett pulled out the desk chair and sat facing her.

"What's going on?"

"That's what I wanted to ask you, actually. How is it coming?"

"We're ready," he told her proudly. "We open the doors for business bright and early tomorrow morning."

"Wonderful. And Jessa?"

"You should see her shop. It's amazing, the kind of place you want to poke around in for hours. She's going to do the Chatams proud with the wedding flowers."

"Yes, I'm sure she is. What I mean is, what about *you and Jessa?*"

Garrett chuckled. Ah, so now they'd come to the point. "Jess and I…we're good, I think. Maybe better than good."

Magnolia smiled. "Things are getting serious then, are they?"

He didn't even try to hold back. "I think so. I hope so. They certainly are for me."

"You've told her, then?"

"Told her?" he echoed uncertainly.

Magnolia looked down at her hands, and her meaning hit him even before she said, "About your past. You *have* mentioned it, haven't you?"

"Well, not exactly. That is…" He meant to tell her. At some point. "We haven't talked about it specifically."

"You'd be wise to tell her yourself before someone else does," Magnolia pointed out gently.

Garrett put a hand to the back of his neck. "I know. You're right. And I have tried. The time's just never been right. I'll tell her as soon as we get past the opening."

Magnolia nodded. "That's good. Very wise. There's no point in upsetting the apple cart now. Once she fully understands, I'm sure she'll be as supportive of you as the rest of us." Rising to her feet then, Magnolia smoothed her gathered skirt with her gnarled hands and stepped gingerly toward the door. "Well, I won't keep you. I know you're tired and want to rest up for your big day. I'm glad we had a moment to talk, though."

Garrett stood and pushed the chair under the desk to give her room to pass. "Me, too. Say a prayer for us."

"Many," she assured him before walking out onto the tiny landing.

Garrett followed her and watched as she made her way down the first two steps. Suddenly he felt compelled to speak. "Mags! I—I mean—"

"Mags will do, my dear, between us," she said, pausing to look up at him over her shoulder, a wry smile in place.

His heart swelling at the allowed intimacy, he stepped closer. "I hope you know...I *trust* you know how deeply I care for you. What I mean is, well, I can't help thinking that I'll be leaving here soon, for good, and I want to be sure that you know I would never disrespect you and..." He found his throat clogged by a big knot and attempted to clear it away as her amber eyes sparkled wetly up at him from the shadowed stairwell. Before he could quite speak again, however, she turned and continued on her way.

"I love you, too," she said.

Humbled and warmed, he watched her descend the few remaining steps, cross the tiny foyer and walk out the door. How God had blessed his once-blighted life by bringing him to this place and these people! Surely, the Father would work out everything else to his benefit.

Now all he had to do was find the courage to tell Jessa everything.

Just as soon as they'd gotten past the grand opening.

He tried to imagine what words he would use, and couldn't

come up with anything that seemed remotely sensible. He wished that Magnolia had given him some tips, but then Mags was so much older than Jessa.

His sister, Bethany, came to mind. She and Chandler would be attending the wedding in a few days, so he'd discouraged her from making the drive, three hours each way, for the opening. That, he decided, had been a mistake. He could be excused for wanting his sister here on one of the biggest, most important days of his life, couldn't he? And after she met Jessa, Bethany could advise him on the best approach to take when telling Jessa about his past. Comforted by that plan, he turned and went into his room. Once there, he closed the door and took out his cell phone.

The grand opening exceeded all of Garrett's expectations. It seemed that the Chatams had recruited their every friend to patronize the Willow Tree shops. Customers were lined up at the nursery door well before time to open it, and they hadn't come just to drink free coffee and eat Hilda's ginger muffins. They exclaimed over the tall, glassed-in area with which Garrett and Dale Bowen had connected the garage and shed, but they hadn't come to gawk, either. They, happily, had come to purchase. Garrett quickly saw that he would be hard-pressed to keep up until the two high-school seniors he'd hired as part-time afternoon employees could arrive. Mags, bless her, jumped in to help out, quickly learning the peculiarities of the electronic cash register, and Garrett realized belatedly that Chester had been loading plants into cars all morning.

When Bethany and Chandler arrived, along with their son Matthew, who was trying determinedly to walk at only ten months of age, Garrett hardly had a moment to greet them, let alone visit. When Chandler started carting out the bulk-

ier plants for customers, Garrett began to realize that he was
going to need full-time assistance on a regular basis.

From what he could tell, Jessa's business was also doing
well. Jessa had called on her friend, Abby, to assist her. A
pleasant woman a decade or so younger than the Chatam sisters, Abby seemed perfectly willing to help out, but she was
definitely frazzled when he and Magnolia, at the latter's firm
insistence, crossed the lot to the floral shop. Bethany stood
at the counter, Matthew on her hip, chatting with Jessa as
Hypatia and Odelia watched expectantly.

"Come! Come, come," Kent urged, waving them over as
soon as Garrett and Magnolia stepped up through the door.

Magnolia all but dragged Garrett to the counter. "Kneel.
Kneel," she directed. "You're too tall."

"No, no! Behind the counter!" ordered a man's voice. Only
then did Garrett see the fellow with the camera. As Bethany moved off, Garrett hurried around to stand beside Jessa,
looping his arm lightly about her shoulders.

"What's going on?" she asked as lights flashed.

"Not sure," he admitted, hearing the shutter click repeat-
edly.

"It's our grand-opening gift!" Odelia exclaimed. "You can
each have a photo to frame and hang over the counter."

Jessa glanced up at him then smiled brightly for the
camera. Garrett pulled her a little closer to his side and did
likewise. Several moments of flashing and clicking later, the
man tucked the camera into a bag and produced a pad and
pencil. He stepped away with Hypatia, jotting down whatever pertinent information he needed. Garrett slipped over
to his sister, who had taken Hunter in charge. He sat on the
floor amongst the adults, laughing as Matthew, who stood in
front of him, gripped his shaggy hair with tiny, eager hands.

"Don't let him hurt you," Bethany instructed.

"He won't," Hunter replied confidently.

Garrett smiled at the two boys playing together and bent his head near his sister's ear. She smoothed back her sleek, dark hair, ready to listen.

"What do you think?" he asked.

Bethany glanced around the shop, and he prepared himself to be a bit more direct, but then she turned a smile on him and said softly, "I like her very much."

Garrett relaxed. "I knew you would."

"So do you," she surmised wisely.

"I need to ask you something."

"Okay."

Before he could speak again, however, the door opened and Chandler poked his head inside. Spying him at once, he said to Garrett, "Better get out here, bro. Someone's trying to buy your potted willow."

"Not the one out front!" Garrett yelped.

"She says she wants something dramatic."

"I have to go," Garrett muttered, and began weaving through the throng. "We'll talk later!"

"No need!" Bethany called, giving him a thumbs-up.

He smiled, glad to have her blessing, but he still needed her advice. As soon as he rescued his willow.

As diplomatically as possible, he denied the woman her prize then proceeded to sell her a pair of pin oaks and an ornamental holly. His teenage helpers arrived, freeing Chester and Chandler but requiring several minutes of Garrett's attention. Then a new wave of customers necessitated the making of a fresh pot of coffee. Before Garrett knew it, the sun had set. He vaguely remembered Bethany waving goodbye a few hours earlier, Matthew asleep on her shoulder.

The boys began straightening the rows of plants in the greenhouse while Garrett turned the sign on the door from Open to Closed. When they had gone, Garrett cleared out the register, amazed at the day's take, and set the timer on the misters. Exhausted, he locked the doors and trudged across the now-empty lot in the deepening gloom of an oncoming night.

The sign in Jessa's window also read Closed, but she hadn't shut the interior door and when he pulled on it, the outer glass door swung open easily. Carrying the bank bag with the day's substantial earnings, he stepped up into the shop just as she tucked a stack of bills into a similar bag. She looked over at him, fatigue pulling down her shoulders and dulling her gaze, but then she burst into laughter. He joined her as he dragged himself to the counter.

"Can you believe it?"

"I have to restock already!" she exclaimed.

"Even if this is three times what I can expect on a normal day," he said, hefting the bag, "I need full-time help."

She nodded her understanding. "I never dreamed business would be this good."

"It's going to be better," he promised, adding softly, "everything's going to be better." Her gaze held his, glowing softly, until his stomach rumbled loudly.

"Sorry! Magnolia brought me a burger for lunch, but I only managed a bite or two of it."

"Same with me," Jessa told him. "I ordered pizza a couple minutes ago."

"Good thinking," Garrett praised. "Where's Hunter?"

"He left with the Chatams earlier. I was just too busy to watch over him. They said they'd get him home again."

Garrett nodded, and while Jessa finished tucking the few unsold arrangements into the cooler in the workroom, he locked the outer doors and turned off the display lights. They had just finished their respective chores and were moving into the house when a knock sounded at the front door.

"That's either Hunter or the pizza," Jessa said, leaving

Garrett to shut and lock the door connecting the shop to the house.

It turned out to be neither. Chester stood on the porch, smiling while the town car idled in the drive. "The misses require your presence for dinner at Chatam House," he announced formally.

Jessa began to protest. "But I've ordered pizza."

"They'll be most disappointed if you don't attend," Chester warned. "Hilda has prepared a special dinner in your honor."

Garrett looked to Jessa and saw agreement in her eyes. "We have to swing by the bank and make deposits," he said to Chester.

"Not a problem," Chester insisted.

"I'll get the bank bags," Garrett told Jessa, handing over his phone. "You can call the pizza shop from the car."

As he settled into the car, it occurred to Garrett that his revelations would have to wait. He wasn't unhappy about that, truth to tell, but he promised himself that he would speak to his sister as soon as possible. Then, after receiving her input, he'd confess all to Jessa. And pray that it didn't change her feelings for the worse.

A special dinner proved to be an understatement, as Jessa learned the instant they stepped through the dining-room door at Chatam House and a rousing cheer went up. It was a real party. A tired-looking Abby was there, along with the carpenter Dale Bowen, as well as several Chatam relations, including little Gilli and her parents, Anna and Reeves Leland, and Kaylie and Stephen Gallow and one of Kaylie's brothers, Morgan, the college professor. Chandler and Bethany, Garrett's very sweet sister, hadn't been able to stay, according to Hypatia.

Given that Bethany and her cowboy husband lived nearly

three hours away, their presence at the opening made a clear testament about their affection for Garrett. Obviously, the feeling was mutual, and Garrett had undoubtedly told his sister that he and Jessa were forming a personal relationship. Bethany had made that clear when she'd smiled at Jessa and said, "I'm so glad you can see past my brother's difficulties to the very fine man that he is."

Jessa wondered about those difficulties, but she hadn't had time then to discuss the matter. Probably Bethany had meant no more than the confusion over the lease. Jessa bit her lip, wishing that she'd felt comfortable enough to invite her sister, Mona, to the opening today, but Mona had caved to pressure and given Wayne information about Jessa and Hunter once before. Jessa simply couldn't take the chance on it happening again. Maybe someday she could contact Mona again, she thought wistfully.

The staff joined everyone else at the dinner table that night, Garrett being one of their own, as Hilda put it. Garrett whispered to Jessa that it was staff preference that kept them from joining the family for dinner every night. Jessa could understand that, given the dignity and formality with which the sisters routinely conducted their meals.

Hubner Chatam, the retired pastor and elder brother of the triplets, spoke a long, detailed blessing over the meal, seeking God's continued blessings on Jessa and Garrett and their respective enterprises. Jessa felt strangely conspicuous afterward. No one, to her knowledge, had ever prayed for her publicly by name before this. She felt as if God's eyes were clearly focused on her for perhaps the first time. Or was it this house and those within it that drew His benevolent gaze?

With the massive dining table extended and filled, the mood became quite jovial and lighthearted. Looking around at the happy faces and knowing that all those smiles were owing in part to her success that day, Jessa wondered how she could have ever believed that she would walk away from this Chatam world and lose all ties with it. She was glad that it hadn't turned out that way. Being here like this was almost like having real family again. And perhaps, she thought, gripping Garrett's hand, that would someday be the case.

Chapter Thirteen

After a couple of hours, Garrett leaned close and murmured, "I don't know about you, but I've about had all the fun I can stand."

Jessa chuckled and sent him a scolding glance, but she agreed. He had to be as exhausted as she was.

For once, Hunter did not sit between them. Instead, he sat to her right, and he obviously didn't like not being privy to the conversation. Leaning forward to look at Garrett, he fairly shouted, "What?"

Most around the table stopped to see what was happening in their little corner, smiles and laughter signaling that they expected it to be something humorous. Garrett cleared his throat.

"I was just telling Jessa that, as lovely as this is, I'm about to fall asleep on my plate. I feel like a puppy with a full belly." Everyone laughed as he patted his middle.

"In that case," said Hypatia, rising to her feet, "I have an announcement to make. Then you two may rest up for another successful day of commerce. We have gifts for you."

"The photos," Garrett surmised. "That was fast."

"No, no, those will come later," Magnolia said with a dismissive wave.

"This is *much* better!" Odelia trilled.

"Our gift to each of you," Hypatia said, "is a quarterly ad in the local newspaper."

Garrett's jaw dropped. Jessa knew he'd priced the ads earlier and found them a bit too expensive. She hadn't wanted to pursue it, and he'd dropped the matter. She realized now that she should've taken the time to tell him why she preferred not to advertise in the newspaper, then perhaps he could have stopped this. As it was, no one here but her knew that Wayne worked for a statewide publication and routinely tracked dozens of Texas newspapers daily. He would pay attention to any advertisement for a new florist shop and perhaps follow up on it. Still, Willow Tree Floral showed no outward connection to her. She wasn't *really* worried—until Hypatia sprung the second half of the surprise.

"But that's not all!" she went on delightedly. "The two of you will be on the front page of tomorrow's newspaper! With a full story about how you met and both came to open your businesses at the same location."

People clapped even as Jessa felt the color drain from her face. Did Wayne scan *every* newspaper? She had no way of knowing that. He'd rarely talked about his work except to complain. *Please, God!* she silently cried.

Garrett wrapped an arm around her shoulders. "Jessa? Honey, are you all right?"

She stared at him dumbly for a moment then realized that voicing her fears now would hurt and dismay the Chatams, who had acted only from kindness. She managed a nod and wan smile.

He pushed back his chair. "You're tired. I'll take you home."

"You're as tired as she is," Magnolia objected. "Chester will drive her."

"Yes," Jessa agreed, getting to her feet. "You rest. I'll see you tomorrow." He seemed disappointed, even troubled, but she didn't want to blight his day with her fears.

"Thank you all so much," she said warmly, taking Hunter by the hand and pulling him up. "I am stunned and flattered by your generosity and good wishes." She squeezed Hunter's hand, saying, "I was just thinking to myself how like family you all seem to us. I so appreciate and *love* you all." She couldn't help looking at Garrett when she said that last.

Quickly bidding everyone a good-night, she got Hunter and herself out of there. Chester, Garrett and Magnolia trailed her, but she simply dispensed smiles and left the latter two standing on the porch. *You're overreacting,* she told herself. *Please God,* she prayed, *let that be the case.*

Uneasy, Garrett watched the taillights of the long sedan as they receded down the drive.

"Now, don't worry," Magnolia said from the darkness at his side. "I made very sure that the newspaper story would cover only the day's events."

"Oh. Thank you," he said, realizing for the first time how damaging it could be if the newspaper dredged up all the old story. "I know you don't like using the Chatam influence."

"What else is it for?" she said dismissively.

"Did she seem all right to you?" he asked.

"Tired," Magnolia said with a shrug.

Garrett shifted around to face her. "You don't think that story could put her in danger, do you?"

Magnolia gasped. "From her ex-husband? That never even occurred to me. But surely it won't matter. I mean, why would her ex have reason to read the *Buffalo Creek Daily Record?*"

"You're right," Garrett agreed, relaxing marginally. "He has no way of knowing that she came here."

"We only wanted to give you both a good start," Magnolia pointed out.

Garrett smiled. "I know that. And if today is any indication, you've done so. In spades."

Magnolia turned back toward the open front door, asking wryly, "Do you still think you'll be working here part-time?"

Sighing, Garrett followed her inside. "I think I'll be putting up a Help Wanted sign first thing tomorrow morning."

Chuckling, she led him down the hallway back to the party. "Hub may have a few names for you. He's seeing more and more people in search of work at the Single Parents Ministry."

"I'll speak to him," Garrett said. "Then I'm done. I'm off to bed while I can still make it that far."

"You go right ahead, dear," Magnolia said, pausing to pat his cheek. "You've earned your rest."

Giving in to impulse, he wrapped his arms around her in a hug. "And you, my lovely, have earned many jewels in your heavenly crown."

"If so," she told him with a smile, "you are definitely one of them."

Day Two proved as exhausting as Day One. Between unloading the new plants he'd ordered, handling customers, updating his computer ledger and just walking the Chatam estate to make sure that nothing needed his immediate attention, Garrett barely had a moment to himself. He managed to pop in on Jessa a couple times, but she was too busy restocking, handling customers and working on the flowers for the wedding to do more than send him a distracted nod. If she seemed worried, he chalked it up to the fact that she was working as hard as he was, but he promised himself that he'd be on guard. Thankfully, one of his teen employees casually mentioned an inexpensive software package that would link his computer and his cash register so he wouldn't have to manually update his ledger.

Garrett bought the software online that evening and installed it for both his business and Jessa's, eating pizza while doing so. Afterward, Jessa pleaded fatigue, so he took himself home, expecting to spend the whole day with her and Hunter on Sunday, starting with church. Instead, he found himself interviewing a prospective employee whom Hubner introduced to him before the worship service.

Billy Champs, the divorced father of twin preschoolers, sported several tattoos, pierced ears and a goatee, but he'd operated his own successful lawn service for years.

"The business suffered after my wife skipped out and left me with two kids to raise alone," Billy said. "You know how it is. The kids come first, even if it means your income drops."

Garrett deduced that Billy had struggled to meet the needs of his family and keep food on the table for nearly three years, but he was now eager to land a steadily paying job that would allow him to pick up his kids from school after they started kindergarten in the fall and spend evenings with them.

"Okay," Garrett told him. "Why don't you come by the nursery after lunch? We'll talk there."

"I'll have to bring the kids, man, but they won't be a problem, I promise."

"I look forward to meeting them," Garrett said before slipping into the worship service late.

After the service, Garrett dropped Jessa and Hunter at Willow Place then drove the triplets to Chatam House. From there, he rode the motorcycle over to a local fast-food drive-through to pick up some burritos for lunch. He, Jessa and Hunter ate on the front porch of the Monroe house, enjoying the warm day and sunshine. They hadn't even gone inside yet when Billy and his kids showed up in a battered SUV.

"Go on," Jessa told Garrett. "Don't worry about us. I'm doing nothing today. This is a true day of rest for me."

"Good," he said, bending to kiss her cheek before walking Billy back to the nursery. While talking to him there, Garrett saw how well he managed his curious children, a girl and a boy.

They were more than a year younger than Hunter, but the three of them seemed to bond instantly and were soon outside pretending that the railroad ties which delineated the boundaries of the parking area were tightropes. Billy managed to give Garrett his attention while keeping an eye on his children at the same time. Garrett made up his mind to hire the fellow. Billy wanted to start right away, so Garrett immediately began his training. Jessa called Hunter inside to clean up for dinner and the Champs children rejoined their father, but even then Billy had questions. Garrett patiently and fully answered each one.

When Garrett went into the house to tell Jessa the good news, he found her nursing a killer headache and wanting nothing more than to crawl into bed. She professed no interest in dinner or anything else except sleep. She worried Garrett by agreeing with his suggestion that he take Hunter home with him for the night. He reluctantly left her, promising not to let Hunter out of his sight, as she anxiously demanded.

After spending the evening with the boy in the small suite, Garrett rose early on Monday morning to tend to some chores around the estate. Then he and Hunter ate breakfast at Hilda's table and carried the same meal to Jessa. She ate mechanically, obviously distracted, but reported that her headache had, mercifully, abated. Garrett sent Hunter out to feed the cat, which had yet to put in an appearance at Chatam House again, and made her sit down at the workbench in the old butler's pantry.

"Honey, what's wrong?"

She gazed up at him with forlorn eyes, but before she spoke, Abby Stringer called out to them from the shop. They went out to find that she had brought with her a middle-age woman named Olive, who hoped for a job.

Sighing, Jessa gave Garrett a wan smile and whispered, "I'm just a little overwhelmed."

He could believe that. "You'd better go talk to this lady then. I'll say a prayer for you. I know you could use some help, too. We'll talk tonight."

Nodding, she pressed a quick kiss to his lips. He smiled to himself, that kiss doing much to relieve his concern, and went out to check on Billy.

Garrett ended the day convinced that Billy was going to prove a great blessing. Jessa seemed less certain about her new helper, Olive, but was willing to give the woman a chance. She started yawning before she could give him many details. He kissed her good-night and took himself off to his bed in the carriage house, pleasantly exhausted. As he drifted toward sleep, the thought flitted through his head that they hadn't had a private moment to talk. Both Magnolia and Bethany had counseled forthrightness, and he knew that was best. Tomorrow, he told himself, would be the day that he would tell her all. He fell asleep before his prayer for favor could fully form in his mind.

Billy had asked for and received permission to bring his kids in with him for a couple hours on Tuesday morning until their grandmother could pick them up, so Garrett knew that Hunter was playing with his new friends. Jessa, of course, would be busy at the floral shop. Garrett felt confident that he wouldn't be missed if he took the morning to mow the front lawn at Chatam House. He started early and finished well before lunch, which gave him time to shower before heading over to Willow Tree Place with a packet of sandwiches prepared by Hilda.

He arrived, feeling that things were finally settling into a workable routine, and noticed that Olive stood out front of the floral shop with her arms folded and her toe tapping. Puzzled by that, he flipped her a little wave as he moved away from the bike toward the shop door, his bag of sandwiches in tow.

"I wouldn't go in there if I was you," she said in a low, disapproving voice. A mannish-looking woman with a square build, short grayish hair and a heavily featured face, she seemed polite but not overly friendly.

Garrett's brow beetled. "Oh? Why is that?" he paused to ask.

"She's got a *personal* customer in there."

"A personal customer?" Garrett echoed uncertainly.

"That's what he said when he came in. Told me to get out because he was her 'personal customer.'"

He? "And you just left?" Garrett growled, hurrying away without waiting for an answer. Sandwiches dropping to the ground, he yanked open the door and virtually leapt through it.

A large, forty-something man with short, dark brown hair leaned across the counter, one hand closed in the front of Hunter's T-shirt. "I'm not telling you again!" he snarled.

At the same time, Jessa cried, "Take your hands off him!"

Garrett didn't wait to hear more. He caught the big man by the shoulder and spun him around. Gold-and-green hazel eyes glared at him from a surprisingly handsome face that was an adult version of Hunter's. Then abruptly, the expression changed from one of angry belligerence to confident affability. Brushing Garrett's hand from the shoulder of his expensive tailored shirt, the man shot his cuffs, straightening them so that the gold cuff links were clearly visible. Obviously, he had some means; yet his ex-wife and child had just as obviously struggled financially. Garrett's opinion of the man dipped even lower.

"Pardon me, friend," the fellow said, certain of his ability to charm. "You've stumbled into a little family drama."

"Is that what you call it?" Garrett asked. He looked to Jessa. "Is this who I think it is?" She nodded, holding Hunter against her. So, the newspaper story has borne bitter fruit, after all. Pushing that matter aside to be dealt with later, Garrett turned back to the unwelcome intruder, who stuck out one hand.

"Wayne Harman," he said, smiling as if this were a social occasion, "Jessa's husband and Hunter's dad."

Possessiveness flared in Garrett. Jessa and Hunter were *his*. He parked his hands at his waist. "You mean Jessa's abusive ex and Hunter's so-called dad, don't you?"

The affable mask slipped briefly, but then Harman injected just the right amount of sadness into his smile. "I can't imagine what she's been telling you."

"That you're divorced for one thing."

"That part's true," Harman acknowledged, looking away. "I'm not happy about it. She may be a compulsive liar, but I still love her." Jessa gasped at that.

"And if she gives you a chance, you'll beat those words right into her, won't you?" Garrett retorted.

Harman gave up the pretense, slashing Garrett with a malicious glance. "Look, she stole my son from me."

"That's not true!" Jessa insisted. "I have full, legal custody of Hunter."

"You know that court hearing wasn't fair!" Harman shouted. "They didn't even give me visitation rights!"

"In other words," Garrett said, "you have absolutely no right to be here."

"Back off, buddy!" Harman bawled, taking a menacing step forward. "This is none of your business."

"Ah, there's the real Wayne Harman," Garrett drawled, standing his ground. "Charm doesn't work, so next you try intimidation. Well, that doesn't cut it with me, either. Get out, and get out now."

Suddenly, Harman threw a punch. Evading that easily, Garrett simply opened his arms and let Harman propel himself into them before throwing them both backward through the door and out onto the ground. He didn't want any scuffle to tear up Jessa's shop, and he hoped that public scrutiny, however slight, would calm Harman, but he'd forgotten about Olive, who screamed like she'd been stabbed and scrambled out of the way. Garrett rolled and came to his feet, prepared to offer Harman a hand up.

Enraged, Wayne Harman slapped Garrett's hand away then staggered to his feet and charged. Garrett popped him on the chin, but the big man shook it off and came back for more. Garrett had no choice but to oblige. It was that or take a beating that would leave Jessa and Hunter even more vulnerable than before. He put every lesson he'd ever learned about eliminating a threat to good use, and he was the only one standing some minutes later when the cops arrived.

Hearing the siren well before the squad car appeared, Garrett turned toward the drive with a sinking feeling. Olive waved energetically at the street, her cell phone in her hand. Obviously, she'd called 911. Gasping for breath, Garrett wiped his bloody lip on his sleeve before turning toward the shop. Jessa and Hunter stood in the doorway.

"I'm sorry, babe," he said, his heart sinking. "The Chatams never intended to hurt anyone with that story. I hoped it would go unnoticed."

"I know," she replied in a small voice. "Me, too."

Her wary gaze snapped to Harman as he groaned and

rolled to his hands and knees. He glanced at the two city police officers, who stood talking to an excitedly chattering Olive. Garrett nodded at Billy as he came out of the nursery to see what was going on. Garrett needed the other man's help in a big way now. His blood chilled as the enormity of his situation hit him. It was so easy to forget the conditions of his parole when his contact with the past consisted of a once-monthly phone call.

Feet crunched on gravel as the officers approached. Harman took the opportunity to collapse on the ground as if lethally wounded and point at Garrett.

"That guy attacked me!"

"That's not true!" Jessa cried, pointing at Harman. "Wayne threw the first punch! And he's here in defiance of a court order."

"I have a right to see my son!" Harman growled.

"Not according to the court," Jessa said, clasping Hunter against her as if fearing Harman would yet try to steal him. "We have a protective order against him."

One officer went to Harman and pulled him to his feet, while the other approached Garrett. "You know the drill," he said.

Shamed, Garrett grit his teeth and turned his back, putting his hands together behind him, while the officer recited his Miranda rights.

"I'm sorry," he said to Jessa again. "I'm so sorry."

The cold bite of steel at both wrists nearly brought him to his knees, but he nodded when asked if he understood his rights. His only consolation was seeing Harman also being fitted with handcuffs. Suddenly, Jessa was at his side. Garrett looked down at her. *Too late.* The words echoed through his mind. *Too late. Too late.* He'd left it all too late.

"I didn't want it to happen like this," he began.

"It wasn't your fault," she said. Looking to the officer, she reiterated the point. "It wasn't his fault! I told you, Wayne threw the first punch."

"Like that matters to this one," the officer scoffed, taking Garrett by the arm. "Just can't resist the violence, can you, Willows? Looks like prison would've tamed that tendency. But, no, it probably made it worse."

"Prison!" Jessa gasped, falling back.

Grief swamped Garrett. Why hadn't he told her, explained? Why did she have to find out this way?

"I was going to tell you," he began.

At the same time, the policeman asked, "You didn't know? He nearly beat a man to death. Served, what, less than eight of a twenty-year sentence?"

Garrett didn't bother answering that. What difference did it make?

Jessa stepped back, shock rounding her eyes and mouth. She shook her head then clamped a hand over her mouth. She felt sick to her stomach

"Jess!" Garrett cried, trying to reach out to her, but the cop yanked him toward the patrol car. "Jessa!" As he was dragged past Olive, he angrily ordered, "Go take care of her!"

Her heavily featured face registered fear, as if she expected him to attack her. Then the officer shoved Garrett into the patrol car, and she finally tottered off toward Jessa. Garrett crammed his too-large feet into the tiny space allotted for them behind the heavy mesh screen separating front seat from back and lifted his hands to the small of his back to make sitting bearable. The door closed, and he pressed his face to the window glass, watching as Jessa retched into the bushes beneath the shop window and Olive awkwardly patted her shoulder while Hunter looked on worriedly.

"Oh, God, help her," Garrett prayed, his eyes filling. "Please help them both!"

He quickly sniffed back his tears as Harman dropped

onto the seat next to him from the opposite side of the car. Harman alternately blamed and threatened him while the officer walked around to the passenger seat, but Garrett kept his eyes on Jessa. The other policeman took brief statements from Olive, Jessa and Hunter, while his partner waited in the car with the arrested men and Harman complained about everything from his discomfort to the court system. Garrett caught Billy's eye and took some comfort in his encouraging nod.

The second cop got in behind the steering wheel and started the engine, turning the car forward into the parking area before backing it around onto the drive again. Garrett tried to make eye contact with Jessa, but not only would she not look at him, she made Hunter turn away, too. Garrett closed his eyes.

"Ex con or ex-husband," Wayne sneered, "wonder which one of us will see her next?"

"You go near her again," Garrett said dully, "and I won't be the only convicted felon she knows. Cops here have you on their radar now."

That shut him up finally. Garrett could only pray that it would be enough to keep her and Hunter safe. Once more, it seemed, he had wasted his heroics and ruined everything that he most wanted to protect.

Chapter Fourteen

She couldn't believe it. Jessa sat numbly on the stool at the counter, trying to make sense of what had happened and all she'd heard, while Olive babbled in the background.

"I knew it was him. I knew he was that boy that took the baseball bat to his step-daddy, so naturally I called 9-1-1 right away." She went on about Garrett's mother and the tragedy of her death, but Jessa couldn't bear to hear any more and shut out the sound of the other woman's voice. Garrett's new hire, Billy, came in.

"What happened?"

"He lied to me," she heard herself saying.

Hunter placed a hand on her arm and laid his head on her lap. She pulled him up until his head lay on her shoulder. After a moment, he began to sob.

"He lied to us," she said, patting his back.

"Will he come back?" Hunter asked in a small, tight voice.

"Wayne?"

"Garrett!"

"I—I don't know."

"But what if Daddy comes back?" Hunter sobbed.

"We'll call the police," she said, trying to reassure him.

"I want Garrett," he wailed.

But Garrett had lied to them.

She still couldn't wrap her mind around the idea of Garrett serving a prison sentence, but the policeman had said he'd probably violated his parole.

Did the Chatams know? she wondered. But of course they knew! And in their gentle, perfect, well-heeled world they had forgiven and overlooked and carried on, never having to consider what harm such violence could do.

Jessa closed her eyes. What had she done? She'd tried to protect her son from one abusive man only to expose him to a dangerously violent one. And she'd broken her own heart in the process.

"God forgive me," she whispered, though she knew that she would never forgive herself. She couldn't even think about forgiving Garrett.

All she could do, she told herself dully, was somehow carry on. She was good at that. She had lots of practice at going on as if nothing horrible had happened. She still had Hunter, after all, and she still had the shop. Wayne was locked away, and Garrett... Garrett could take care of himself.

She had a son to care for and a home to provide and... flowers to arrange. She would manage. Somehow, she would manage.

Gingerly easing the long, narrow box of flowers from the back of the rented van, Jessa balanced its saggy middle on one knee. Adjusting her hold, she turned toward the side door of the sanctuary at Downtown Bible Church. The heavy door opened and Magnolia Chatam stepped through it, holding it wide.

"May I be of assistance?"

Sighing inwardly, Jessa managed as much of a smile as she was able. She had avoided Magnolia and her sisters at

Chatam House earlier when delivering the flowers for the reception, not that she blamed them for alerting Wayne to her location. They had meant no harm and only wanted to help. Besides, it was bound to have happened sooner or later. No, Wayne was not the issue.

In fact, after speaking at length with the local police department, Jessa had decided that she and Hunter were going to stay in Buffalo Creek and trust the police to enforce the protection order against Wayne. After cooling his heels in jail for forty-eight hours before being allowed to post bail, surely he had realized that he had no choice except to stay away.

She wouldn't think about Garrett. She *couldn't*. Not yet. Which was why she had done her best to avoid the Chatams. She couldn't bear to think that all her worst fears had come true, that he had lied to her, or at the very least omitted vital information. She couldn't bear to know how foolish she'd been. She had dared to believe, if ever so slightly, in happily ever after, and she couldn't face the fact that it was not to be hers. Because he had gone to prison, served time in prison. For violence. For beating a man nearly to death.

But that was on Garrett, not the Chatams.

Steeling herself, she nodded at Magnolia. "Thanks. I don't want to leave anything in the van too long in this heat."

The weather had turned quite warm lately, as if her learning the truth about Garrett had sucked all the mildness and comfort out of the atmosphere. Jessa turned off that thought and carried the box through the door, leaving Magnolia to go to the van. For several minutes, they passed each other coming and going as they carried the floral decorations into the cool sanctuary. When all the flowers were inside the building, Jessa began to arrange them as needed.

She started with the pew bows then placed arrangements at strategic locations before turning her attention to the most important job. A white latticed arch had been erected in front of the altar and a small white pedestal stood to one side, topped by a large, intricately carved unity candle and two tapers, one a pale lilac color and the other a delicate gray. A long, white satin runner waited to be unrolled up the center aisle. Jessa placed arrangements at the feet of the arch then began weaving long chains of spring flowers through the lattice with the aid of a small stepladder that Magnolia had produced and now held for her.

Jessa worked in silence, concentrating on the job at hand, so that she wouldn't bruise or dislodge any of the blooms. The sudden sound of Magnolia's voice jolted her.

"He was trying to protect her, you know."

Jessa didn't have to ask who *he* was, but she automatically asked, "Her?"

"His mother. Shirley."

Jessa knew, of course, that Garrett's mother had been a victim of spousal abuse and that she was now deceased. Beyond that she knew nothing else. "What about her?"

"Her husband, Doyle, Garrett's stepfather, beat her mercilessly. It had been going on a long while, but that time, he put her in the hospital. Garrett only wanted to stop him from doing it again."

Jessa shuddered, recalling the bits and pieces that she'd heard. "They say Garrett used a baseball bat." Her stomach turned over at the thought.

"Yes. The same bat Doyle had used to break Shirley's ribs, wrist and jaw."

Jessa gulped and closed her eyes. That did change things. A little. Still…

"Garrett was young, barely twenty-one," Magnolia went on, "and understandably angry. He didn't know what else to do. He was afraid that Doyle would kill her. And Doyle did. While Garrett was in prison."

Jessa gasped and looked down at Magnolia. "His stepfather murdered his mother?"

"With his bare hands."

Jessa squeezed her eyes closed. That poor woman. Poor Garrett. She shook her head, pointing out, "Then it was all pointless, wasn't it?"

"Yes," Magnolia agreed, "and Garrett realized it. That's why, when Shirley refused to press charges against Doyle and went back to him, Garrett pled guilty to felony assault charges and let himself be sent to prison. He thought it was better to be locked away than to stand by helplessly and watch his mother suffer. He didn't feel he could trust himself if—when—Doyle beat her again."

Jessa paused, shaken by the thought of the despair that Garrett must have felt when his mother willingly returned to her abuser. But that didn't change one important fact. "He should have told me."

"Yes, he should have," Magnolia agreed, nodding, "and he intended to."

Jessa shook her head, tears gathering in her eyes. He could have told her that day when he'd first explained his mother's situation.

"He told me that he'd tried to tell you and couldn't do it," Magnolia went on.

Suddenly, Jessa remembered that day in the rose arbor, when he'd seemed to have something on his mind.

"I imagine he was afraid you'd reject him," Magnolia said.

What if he had told her that day? Jessa asked herself, but she already knew the answer. If he'd told her about going to prison that day, even why, then they wouldn't be here now. She'd have run from him and Chatam House as quickly as she could. She'd never have opened the shop. Wayne would never have found her and Hunter, and they would be...where? She couldn't even imagine.

"Then," Magnolia was saying, "after you agreed to share the property with him, everything happened so quickly. You were both so terribly busy…I don't think he had a chance."

Pulling in a deep breath, Jessa tried to clear her head, muttering, "I have work to do." She finished the weave and backed down off the stepladder, her mind whirling with information and recriminations.

"Garrett paid for his mistake," Magnolia told her insistently, "and paid dearly. If I'd known about the plea bargain in time, I wouldn't have allowed it, frankly. But Garrett was too ashamed to tell me. He had never let on what was happening in his mother's house. And he was right about Doyle Benjamin. He knew that he could do nothing to prevent Doyle from beating Shirley again, so he got as far away from the situation as he could. Nearly three years later, when they found Shirley, she was so severely beaten that she was unrecognizable."

Jessa caught her breath against a sob, asking shakily, "What happened to Doyle?"

"He was convicted of first-degree murder. Garrett testified at his trial. He said on the stand that he had failed to protect his mother. I think, ultimately, that's why he pled guilty to the charges that Doyle filed against him, not because Doyle didn't deserve the beating that Garrett gave him—which was much less severe than you may think, certainly less severe than what Doyle did to Shirley—but because ultimately it did nothing to protect his mother. You see, that's the difference between Doyle and Garrett. Doyle was an abuser. Garrett is a protector. Now he could go back to prison for trying to protect you and Hunter."

He *had* tried to protect them, and he hadn't thrown the first punch. Realizing that she had much to think about, Jessa bowed her head. *Oh, Lord, help me judge rightly,* she prayed.

I don't know what to think or what to do. Please don't let me do the wrong thing just because my heart tells me it's right!

Lifting her chin, she said to Magnolia, "I need to get back to the shop."

"Of course," Magnolia conceded. "Just please remember that he loves you."

He loves you. The words echoed in Jessa's heart. She shuddered at the sweet pain of them.

Magnolia sighed and turned to look around the room. "It's lovely, just as the ballroom at the house is lovely. You've done an exceptional job. I trust we'll see you at the wedding later."

"Oh," Jessa hedged, "I—I don't know."

"But you must," Magnolia urged, "you and Hunter both. Otherwise, Ellie and the rest of us will be so very disappointed."

Jessa wanted to ask if Garrett would be there, if he had been released from jail, but she couldn't bear to think of him sitting alone in a jail cell instead of attending the wedding with the rest of them and she didn't trust herself to speak of him any longer.

"We'll try," she finally said, wondering if she had time to buy a dress.

"I'll send someone for you, shall I?" Magnolia pressed. "I'm sure my nephew Morgan wouldn't mind giving you and Hunter a ride."

Jessa gave in. "Yes. All right. Thank you."

"Excellent. I'll have him at Willow Tree Place about a quarter to six this evening."

Nodding, Jessa dusted off her hands and left Magnolia standing there in the sanctuary, staring at the cross on the altar.

Drying his sweaty palms on the jacket of the tuxedo that Magnolia had insisted on purchasing for him, Garrett paced the foyer of the church. He couldn't believe that Asher had managed to get him released in time for the wedding. It wouldn't last, of course. Garrett knew very well that he was almost surely headed back to prison, but at least he had this one final opportunity.

He'd thought about this for hours on end, seeing with his mind's eye Wayne Harman's handsome face and glittering smile. Worse, he remembered how his mother had declared, "Never again!" then gone right back for more. Instinct told him that Jessa would not be so foolish, but fear insisted that anything was possible. Had he made Harman seem pathetic and contrite, as he had Doyle? If so, Jessa could decide to give the marriage another try. Thankfully, Garrett had one more opportunity to save someone he loved, and he couldn't blow it.

He'd thought of phoning her, but she could always hang up, and she might tear up a letter without reading it. No, this had to be done in person. He would accept her rejection and scorn if she would just *listen,* and he would forever be grateful to Asher for making this one last chance possible. What other attorney would bother showing up in court on the very day of his wedding, let alone insist that the hearing take place?

Garrett prayed—again—that Jessa would actually attend the wedding as Magnolia believed and that she would hear him out. When the heavy door opened a few moments later and she preceded Hunter and Morgan Chatam into the soaring foyer, Garrett thanked God, his voice echoing around the immediate space before he'd realized that he'd spoken aloud. Jessa checked her steps, her gaze falling on him then instantly sweeping away.

She looked lovely in a simple marigold yellow dress with fluttering sleeves and a matching ribbon tied at her slender waist. He felt a spurt of pleasure because she'd finally worn something that did her justice. Her long hair had been rolled into a heavy chignon at the nape of her neck, leaving lacy layers to frame her lovely face. Garrett's heart burst with love. And fear.

Morgan ushered Hunter away as Garrett hurried to intercept Jessa. He smiled at the boy but didn't try to approach him, fearing that his mother would be displeased. She drew up but averted her gaze from his.

"I won't keep you," he told her quietly, "and I won't apologize because I don't expect you to forgive me. I just have one thing to say. Please don't go back to him."

Her gaze slashed upward. "What?"

"I beg you," Garrett said urgently. "He's charming, and he's handsome. And he's dangerous. Please don't be fooled."

"You think I might go back to Wayne?" she asked, tilting her head.

"I can see how persuasive he might be, and I know you're disappointed in me," Garrett told her. "I don't blame you for that, but please don't put yourself in danger again just because I've disillusioned you. Chances are I'm on my way back to prison, and I can live with that. But I can't live with the idea of losing someone else I love to an abuser. Promise me you won't go back to him."

"I promise," she said softly. "It's the very last thing I would do. In fact, I've filed another protective order against him here."

Relief swamped Garrett. He let out a breath that he hadn't even realized he'd been holding. "Thank you," he said, backing away. "That's good. Thank you for telling me. I—I just want you to be safe, you know. I would do anything to—" Breaking off before he embarrassed himself by going down on his knees and begging her forgiveness, he turned and swiftly strode away.

He could face whatever came now. So long as he had not

destroyed her faith in her own judgment and left her at the mercy of a master manipulator, he could manage anything. The total destruction of his dreams, the complete pulverization of his heart meant nothing compared to her well-being. He would pay that price and more, so long as she and Hunter were safe.

Now he could turn his mind to other things, like what to do about Willow Tree Nursery. Billy, God bless him, had kept things going. Garrett had briefly broached the idea of leaving Billy in possession of the place with Magnolia, but she had balked, saying that was not necessary. Garrett only knew that he didn't want to leave Billy without an income or Jessa without a partner. It was a quandary that he would lay before Asher, as soon as that good man returned from his honeymoon—and not before. He could stay out of jail that long, at least. Asher had seen to it.

Walking into the sanctuary, Garrett hurried to take his place beside Magnolia. As the stringed quartet played sweet, lilting music, he looked to the altar beyond the flowered arch, and his gaze fell on the gilded cross that stood there. For the first time, really, he had an inkling of the depth of love that had driven Christ to the cross.

He was no martyr himself, no savior. Everything he'd done had backfired in the most horrific of ways.

But let it backfire on me alone, Lord, he prayed. *Never on those I love. Bethany and Mags, little Matthew, Hunter and Jessa, they deserve only joy. I'll take everything I deserve and more, if You'll only spare them.*

Music wafted in lovely dips and swells as Jessa slowly sank down onto the pew beside her son. She had reclaimed him from Morgan, who had patiently and politely waited for her just inside the sanctuary door. A shake of her head had sent him down to the family pew while she and Hunter took a place near the back of the great room. She nodded to the usher who had escorted her, and he turned to retrace his steps. Hunter snuggled up next to her, looking handsome in his new suit. He'd had a haircut, and the shorter style made him look so grown-up. Or was it the solemn expression on his face?

He grieved for Garrett, she knew, her gaze wandering of its own accord to the back of Garrett's dark head. She'd seen the hurt in his eyes when she'd explained that she didn't know when or if they'd see Garrett again. She saw the way he yearned to be there with Garrett and the Chatams now. She fought that urge herself, fearing greater pain in the long run if she went to Garrett now. He had said himself that he would likely return to prison. She couldn't subject her son to that. And yet…

I can't live with the idea of losing someone else I love to an abuser.

Someone I love.

She closed her eyes against the bittersweet memory of that, all the more poignant because he hadn't seemed to realize what he'd said. She mentally scolded herself for coming to the wedding in the first place. Romance filled the very air that she breathed. And cut her heart to ribbons. It was all she could do to sit there and take it. Yet, she hadn't been able to stay away.

Relieved when the ceremony began, Jessa tried to concentrate on what was taking place around her. The music stopped, and the ushers unfurled the aisle cloth by holding onto a cord attached to a small dowel inserted into the end of the roll of fabric as they walked up the aisle from front to back. The music began again, a new piece that Jessa didn't recognize. Little Gilli Leland fairly skipped along the aisle cloth a moment later, looking adorable in her fluttery pale lilac gown, a crown of spring flowers in her curly hair. She strewed silk rose petals as she went, flicking them from a tiny white basket. As soon as she reached the altar, she ran to join her parents in their pew.

Asher's sisters came next, first a blonde, Petra, whom Jessa knew only by name, followed by Dallas. Oddly, the pale lilac gown complemented Dallas's carroty-red hair. Both young women were slender and striking, perfect foils for the groomsmen, Asher's tall, lean brother, Phillip, and cousin, Chandler, either of whom could have graced the covers of fashion magazines, in black and pale gray. Asher himself, with his graying chestnut hair, looked dashing and dignified in his severe tuxedo with a silver-on-gray brocade vest and gray silk tie.

Ellie, as predicted, took everyone's breath away, Asher's especially. He seemed to be restraining himself from charging up the aisle to claim her. The gown showed off Ellie's voluptuous figure in the most elegant fashion imaginable. The delicate gray embroidery of the diaphanous veil perfectly complemented the unusual slate-gray color of her full, curly hair. She looked like a movie star in an old film.

Kent wept openly, dabbing his face with a folded handkerchief, as he escorted his granddaughter down the aisle. He'd chosen a lilac bowtie and matching vest to accent his tuxedo. Odelia, decked head-to-toe in pale pink, from the bow in her hair to the bows on her feet, waved her own hankie at him as they passed by, her dangling pink crystal earrings shimmering in the candlelight. She clapped a hand to the big bow on her chest when, in response to the pastor's question concerning who gave this woman's hand in marriage, Kent answered, "Her future grandmother and I."

Everyone else *aahed* or chuckled, except perhaps Magnolia, who seemed to be rolling her eyes. Her hair had been done in a French braid with the tail tucked under, and she wore a stylish mauve silk. Garrett wrapped his long arm around her slender shoulders, squeezing lightly and whispering into her ear. She laughed, briefly laying her gray head upon his shoulder.

Jessa bit her lip and looked away. Mags would be crushed if Garrett went back to prison. Crushed. The rest of the ceremony passed in a blur. Jessa let herself hover on the periphery of it, reluctant to see or hear too much. The dreamy romance of it all hurt her, literally. She remembered her wedding to Wayne. Though modest and small in comparison, she'd had such high hopes for the future. Wayne had seemed so very *satisfied.* Why hadn't she realized that wasn't enough? Hopeful and satisfied could not compare with the kind of love that Ellie and Asher so obviously shared, the kind of love that she wanted to share with Garrett and now never would.

Memories bombarded her: Garrett smiling patiently at her son, Hunter laughing up at him, Garrett sitting beside her on the arbor bench, reaching for her hand at the table, holding her chair after surprising her with a candlelit dinner, working, working, working to make Willow Tree Place a reality, Garrett folding the bedcovers beneath her son's chin. Garret kissing her, his strong arms holding her close, making her feel so safe and so loved and so wanted. For the first time, she realized just how different her feelings for Garrett were from her early feelings for Wayne.

"You may kiss your bride."

The pastor's announcement, echoing so closely her thoughts, snagged Jessa's attention. She focused on the front of the sanctuary, watching as Asher reverently folded back the front of Ellie's veil and bent his head, smiling. Ellie lifted up onto her toes and twined her arms about his neck. Love poured off the two of them, flowing through the room, filling it. Jessa laughed through her tears, so happy for them, unbelievably sad for herself.

As soon as the newlyweds swept from the room, Jessa

grabbed Hunter's hand and rushed out into the aisle. Finding an inconspicuous corner of the foyer, she stood there, Hunter's hand clasped in hers, and gradually brought herself under control. When Kaylie, the Chatams' niece, and her tall, blond husband, Stephen Gallow, wandered by on the edge of the milling throng that crowded into the space, she caught sight of Jessa and stopped.

"There you are! Can we offer you a ride to the reception?"

Jessa shook her head. She'd rather have her fingernails plucked out than attend the wedding reception and was actively considering walking home from here. It couldn't be more than ten blocks. Kaylie, however, seemed disinclined to take no for an answer and immediately pulled out her cell phone.

"I'll text Morgan to let him know you're with us," she said, thumbs tapping the tiny keyboard. "Stephen, take them to the car. I'll join you in a moment."

Gallow dutifully kissed his wife's cheek, smiled at her absent smile and lifted a hand in invitation to Jessa. Hunter slid to the big man's side and looked up at him.

"Is wedding cake like birthday cake?" he asked.

"Better," Stephen told him, bending low.

"Yum," Hunter said softly, rubbing his abdomen.

Jessa stared at him bleakly for a moment, but she couldn't deny him the wedding cake that Hilda had discussed so many times while they were at Chatam House. He was missing enough already. She would just have to bear up so he could see his friends and eat that cake.

All right, Lord, she prayed silently, following Hunter and Stephen Gallow out of the building, *You're in charge now. I can't think anymore. All I can do is feel. You'll just have to work out everything as You see fit. I give up.*

Chapter Fifteen

Kaylie met them on the sidewalk, the ends of her pale blue chiffon wrap fluttering languidly in the evening breeze. They hurried through the dusk to Stephen's expensive luxury sedan and minutes later stepped out onto the grass at Chatam House, where they'd parked at the direction of none other than Garrett Willows himself. Jessa didn't try to stop Hunter when he darted across the yard to throw his arms around Garrett's legs.

With an apologetic glance in her direction, Garrett stooped and swept the boy up in a hug. They spoke briefly then Garrett set him on his feet again and sent him off with a hand pressed to the center of his back.

"Lemon and raspberry!" Hunter exclaimed, grabbing her hand and all but dragging her toward the house.

"What?"

"Lemon and raspberry filling," he said, "on the cake. And white icing. With all kinds of fancy stuff."

Jessa couldn't help smiling; his enthusiasm was positively infectious. "You have to eat dinner first, you know," she warned.

Hunter sighed. "Yeah, I know. Garrett said."

Garrett said. That was all it took for Hunter.

But what about what Garrett *hadn't* said?

What about what he'd done?

Long ago.

Trying to protect his mother.

Suddenly, she wondered what God was doing. Whatever it was, she decided, following Hunter into the house that had been their sanctuary, it had to be better than what she'd managed on her own. A wave of something very akin to homesickness hit her, but she knew that her yearning was not for that suite of rooms upstairs. It was for the heart and, yes, the arms of the one man in the world who, she now knew without doubt, loved her. A man on his way back to prison.

It helped that everyone was so kind. The Chatam sisters embraced both her and Hunter warmly, thanked them for coming, gushed over the flower arrangements and saw the two of them situated at a table with Gilli Leland and her parents. Reeves and Anna went out of their way to make them welcome and introduced them to everyone who passed by, always making note of Jessa's involvement with the decorations.

Anna's grandmother joined them, as did Reeves's mother and twenty-one-year-old twin half-sisters, Harmony and Lyric. Though identical, the twins could not have been more different. Lyric, a cellist and pianist according to her mother, put Jessa in mind of a young Grace Kelly with her ice-blond hair, dark amber eyes and classic style. Harmony, on the other hand, had sprayed shocking streaks of purple in her long hair. A tiny diamond stud twinkled in one nostril, and her eyes were heavily lined with kohl. She informed Jessa that she played guitar and keyboard, demonstrating with hands garbed with fingerless, fishnet gloves. Jessa got the feeling that her parents endured more than supporting her interests. Both girls demonstrated their Chatam heritage with dainty, feminine clefts in their dainty, feminine chins.

Garrett sat at a table with the Chatam sisters, when he wasn't up rushing around to see to one task or another. The meal was extraordinary: a wide variety of appetizers, followed by a buffet of eye-of-the-round and pork-loin roasts, broiled medallions of sweet potato and too many vegetable dishes to count. The cake was a towering masterpiece decorated with candied violets and silver nonpareil. Half of it was filled with lemon, half with raspberry. Anna saw to it that Hunter received a "joint" piece so that he got some of each, much to his delight, as well as a small chunk of chocolate-cherry groom's cake. He watched the goings-on with interest, but in truth, he was there for the cake—and Garrett.

Several times Hunter jumped up and ran after Garrett, obediently returning to his mother moments later. Eventually, the stringed quartet on the performance stage at the far end of the ballroom departed and a more lively set of recorded popular music began to play. Gilli proclaimed that she was going to dance and literally grabbed Hunter by the coat sleeve, pulling him to his feet. Reeves and Anna just laughed, so Jessa didn't interfere.

Hunter looked at Gilli like she'd grown a second head, but he went along. By the time they reached the empty space in front of the small stage, a number of other children, mostly girls, were already spinning and twirling. A few of them even moved in time with the music. Hunter stood on the periphery for a while. Then he began to tentatively pump his arms. After a moment, he rocked back on one heel. The next thing Jessa knew, he'd executed a neat spin. Gilli tried it and bumped into him. Recognizing his superior spinning ability, Hunter ventured out to demonstrate it, much to the delight of the adults around Jessa's table.

Harmony popped up to join the children on the impromptu dance floor. Soon they followed her like a flock of ducklings as she taught them one move after another. If her spike-heeled half boots and incongruous evening wear, a threadbare denim jacket worn over a long, chiffon sheath, confused Hunter, he gave no sign of it, laughing and following along with surprising dexterity and rhythm.

Jessa relaxed and let Dorinda Chatam Latimer explain all the family connections. Jessa suspected that Dorinda's animation stemmed more from a desire to deflect attention from Harmony's behavior than Jessa's interest. After several minutes, Jessa glanced routinely at the dance floor but didn't immediately sight Hunter. Harmony, she saw, now chatted with another young woman.

Jessa turned her full attention to the laughing, gyrating mass of children, but she did not find Hunter among them. Fear threaded through Jessa's chest, even as she told herself that he'd almost certainly gone off to speak to Garrett. Rising, she murmured an excuse and went in search of one or both of them. A quick survey showed her no sign of either Hunter or Garrett, but she found the latter as soon as she stepped out into the hallway. They almost collided, in fact.

His hands came up to grasp her shoulders, steadying her. "Whoa!" His blue, blue eyes gazing into hers, he tilted his head. "Is everything okay?"

"Have you seen Hunter?"

"Yeah, he's dancing with the other kids. Pretty good, too."

"No. No, he's not. I thought maybe he'd come to see you."

Garrett's expression flashed from pleasure to unease. "I haven't seen him since the music changed, babe, but we'll find him. Come on."

Grasping her hand, he pulled her toward the forward set of pocket doors, which opened nearer the performance area where the children danced. A mere moment was all they required to see that Hunter had not rejoined the group. Garrett caught Chester by the sleeve as he came through the doorway with a tray of dirty dishes.

"Go around and check the gentlemen's restroom for Hunter. He's missing."

Nodding, Chester placed the tray on a folding stand next to the door and hurried away. Garrett towed Jessa into the ballroom and right into the midst of the children.

"Anyone see where Hunter Pagett went? His mom's looking for him."

Gilli answered. "He went to play hide-and-seek with the man."

"What man?" Jessa asked, her heart in her throat.

Gilli shrugged and pointed at the very door through which they had just entered. "I dunno. He did this." She made a motion with her hand, the kind someone would make to encourage another's approach. Jessa's breath snagged in her throat. Wayne wouldn't be foolish enough to try to snatch Hunter now, would he?

"What did Hunter do?" Garrett had the presence of mind to ask.

Gilli pointed to the stage, which could be hidden behind a false wall and opened onto the music room between the ballroom and the library. "He went that way to hide."

Jessa's heart plummeted to her toes. "He would only hide from Wayne," she said urgently. Garrett jerked out his cell phone and thrust it into her hands.

"Call 9-1-1."

He raced off in the direction Hunter had gone. Jessa punched in the numbers with shaking hands. She was talking to the dispatcher when Magnolia appeared at her elbow.

"Jessa?"

Lifting a finger to delay any comment, Jessa turned and walked into the hallway while still speaking to the dispatcher. Magnolia paced her.

"I'm telling you that my ex-husband was seen trying to entice my son to come to him when he's not supposed to be anywhere near either of us," Jessa said. "We have a valid protective order that he's already violated once recently. Now my son is missing, and I need help to find him!" The dispatcher asked where they were. "We're at Chatam House. The address is—"

Magnolia took the phone right out of her hand and spoke into it herself. "This is Magnolia Chatam. I want as many police cars and officers here as you can manage. Immediately!"

Jessa threw a kiss at Magnolia's cheek and rushed off in the same general direction as Garrett. She met Chester in the foyer.

"He's not there, ma'am, and also not in the kitchen."

Nodding, Jessa sprinted for the door. She yanked it open. Chester caught it and held it as she rushed through. He followed on her heels. The sounds of raised voices came from somewhere to their right, one of them Hunter's.

"Let me go! I won't go with you! Let go!"

Jessa and Chester dashed across the porch, down the steps and along the walkway to the porte cochere in time to see Garrett run across it into the darkness beyond, where the murky shape of a man raised his hand to a child.

"I'll teach you to hide from me!"

The blow landed with a sickening thud and knocked Hunter onto his backside. Instantly Garrett hurtled his body at Wayne, shouting, "Run, Hunter!"

Hunter scrambled up and darted back toward the house—straight into his mother's grateful arms.

"Thank God," she gasped. "Thank God!" And thank Garrett. Again.

While the two struggling men rolled on the ground, other people arrived, Magnolia, Reeves and Asher among them. Garrett and Wayne got to their feet. Realizing that they'd drawn a crowd, Garrett admonished Wayne to calm down, but instead Wayne threw a punch, which Garrett avoided. Jessa watched as Garrett held up his hands, indicating that he wouldn't fight back, but Wayne took swipes at him anyway.

"You need to get out of here before the police arrive, Wayne!" Jessa shouted, hoping for Garrett's sake to avoid a repeat of the last time they'd fought. But even then flashing lights appeared on the street. Soon they would turn up the drive.

"Not without my son!" Wayne bawled.

"Man, you have to know that's not happening," Garrett reasoned. "Why do you want to ruin all your lives by stealing him from his mother, anyway?"

"She deserves to have her life ruined!" Wayne shouted. "She left me!"

"Because you abused her!"

"I didn't abuse her," Wayne scoffed. "I only smacked her when she made me. She's got to learn obedience! She's got to learn her place!"

Jessa sighed and shook her head, knowing that Wayne would not listen to reason.

"You're sick," Garrett told him. "You need a major healing in mind and soul, man, and it looks to me like God's been trying to work that in you and you won't let Him."

"Don't preach at me!" Wayne bawled, connecting with a solid roundhouse to the shoulder.

Garrett fell back, and Wayne followed, trying a chop from the left. Stepping in, Garrett knocked him off his feet with a blow that caught Wayne in the throat. "Stay down!" he warned as cops suddenly swarmed the area.

One officer went straight to Garrett, who breathed a great sigh and hung his head. The policeman grabbed one of Garrett's wrists. Jessa opened her mouth to protest, but Asher beat her to it.

"Wait!" Asher called, striding forward. He pointed at Garrett, saying, "This man prevented a kidnapping. He's done nothing wrong. Even after he stopped that man from making off with a child in violation of a protective order, he did his best to avoid a brawl. You have no reason to arrest him."

"It's our policy," the policeman began. Asher cut him off, clapping a hand to Garrett's shoulder.

"I am this man's attorney, and I'm telling you that you're making a mistake. We all saw what happened." He pointed at Wayne. "That man sneaked onto these premises in the middle of *my* wedding reception in order to kidnap that child." He pointed to Hunter, now clasped safely in Jessa's arms. She nodded in an effort to underscore Asher's words. Magnolia stepped up to her side.

"He's done it again," she said softly. "Garrett has risked his own freedom, without a thought for himself, to protect another. But that's what he does. Don't you see? He's a protector, not an abuser."

"I see," Jessa whispered, nodding as a policeman hauled a handcuffed Wayne to his feet. At the same time, Asher and the first officer left Garrett standing alone in the middle of the yard and walked to a patrol car.

Magnolia squeezed Jessa's forearm. "I knew you would."

Jessa tossed her a faint smile as Asher and the policeman approached. Asher had out his cell phone and the policeman carried a camera.

"I want Hunter's injuries well documented," Asher explained. Jessa bent to look closely at her son. He already had the beginnings of an ugly bruise on his cheek.

"Oh, sweetie," she crooned, suddenly near tears.

"It's okay, Mom," he said huskily. "Garrett got here in time."

And he had. He truly had. She turned her tearful gaze in his direction as both Asher and the policeman snapped photos of Hunter. Garrett stood alone, one hand braced at his waist, the other clapped to the nape of his neck. He'd tugged his dirty white cummerbund into place and brushed off his sleeves.

Magnolia went to him, and they spoke for a moment. Then he shook his head, kissed her cheek and made a shooing motion. She turned toward the house and began encouraging the crowd to return to the festivities. They slowly did so, breaking off in twos and threes to wander back inside.

Jessa watched as the police put Wayne into the backseat of a squad car. Here and there, officers took statements and made notes. Asher patted Hunter on the head.

"You don't have to worry about him anymore," Asher promised Jessa, jerking an elbow at Wayne. "I know the judge in this case well, and there won't be any more bail. His Honor takes a dim view of attempted kidnapping. It'll be a long time before Harman has another chance of any kind to get at either of you. Hopefully, by that time, he'll have learned his lesson. If not…" He glanced at Garrett. "I think you'll be safe."

Suddenly, Hunter tore away from Jessa and ran to Garrett, nearly knocking him over with the force of his embrace. Garrett patted his back and ruffled his hair, but still Hunter held on. Jessa knew just how he felt. In some ways, it was like waking from a confusing dream to a clear and certain reality, where all doubts had vanished. She wanted to hold on to that reality and never let it go, but she hung back, allowing Hunter his moment with Garrett. Asher squeezed her hand and left them there, making his way toward the house. A minute or two later, the last police car pulled away, and just the three of them remained.

Garrett turned toward the house, the boy still plastered to his side. They walked to Jessa, who fell in next to them, one hand going to the back of her son's head.

"Thank you," she said in a wobbly voice, trying to smile.

Garrett nodded and walked on. "I'm just glad we were in time."

They reached the shadows of the porch, and there, Garrett paused.

"You two go on in. I think I'll stay here for a little while." Turning, he sat on the edge of the porch, his feet on the steps, and sighed.

"What will you do?" Jessa asked, more in control of herself now. She slid an arm around Hunter's shoulders, assuring herself once more of his safety.

"Pray," Garrett answered succinctly, dropping his head into his hands.

Jessa looked down at Hunter and read the same concern in his face that she was feeling. "In that case," she said, walking back to Garrett, "we'll stay."

She sat down on his right. Hunter went around and sat down on Garrett's left. They each lifted a hand to his back. Suddenly, Garrett made a sound somewhere between a gasp and a sob. Jessa's heart melted.

"Oh, my darling," she crooned, laying her cheek against his shoulder, her eyes leaking tears. "I'm sorry. I was wrong to be angry with you."

"No," he choked out. "You were right. I should've told you before you agreed to share the Monroe place with me."

"Then I wouldn't have," she admitted. "And it's not the Monroe place anymore. It's Willow Tree Place. It's *our* place."

Garrett patted the hand that she'd placed upon his shoulder, then sucked in a deep breath and lifted his head, rubbing his hands over his face. "I thought I'd be in the back of that squad car now."

"Thank God that didn't happen!" she told him.

He nodded and said, "It still could, you know. I'm on parole and—"

"We'll cross that bridge when we come to it," Jessa interrupted, "together. And meanwhile, we'll pray."

Garrett chuckled and laid his head against hers, whispering, "I love you, you know." He turned to squeeze Hunter. "And you."

Hunter reached up to hook an arm around Garrett's neck.

"I love you, too," Jessa said, calmly and clearly. "We both do."

Garrett laughed, sort of, and declared, "Thank God!" He bowed his head then and began to pray. "Father God, we thank You. We're safe and together, and You've shown us that's all that truly matters. Thank You for letting us get to Hunter in time. Thank You for Asher and his efforts. For Billy, who's kept things going, and Willow Tree Place and Mags and the other misses…"

He went on enumerating their blessings until Hunter piped up with, "And wedding cake."

They all laughed then, joy settling in to cover the fear of what might have happened and what still could. Jessa placed it silently in God's hands and vowed simply to feel, allowing herself to be swept along on a tide of love so fierce that it blotted out all fear.

Eventually, they rose to rejoin the party, arriving just in time for Jessa to catch the bridal bouquet that she herself had made. When Garrett slipped his hands around her waist to pull her against him, knowing smiles traveled around the room. Jessa added her own to them then shared it with Magnolia, who nodded in silent approval.

Whatever future God deemed appropriate and best for Garrett Willows, he would live it far from alone.

Epilogue

The first Monday of June dawned bright and hot. As Garrett led Jessa up the steps of Chatam House by the hand, she fanned herself with the other, but then she laughed, and gratitude swamped him once more. Asher and Magnolia went ahead. Asher opened the door and held it, smiling as they passed through.

Everyone had gathered in the front parlor, including a sizable portion of the Chatam family, Chandler and Bethany, of course, and nearly all of Hub's family, excepting only Bayard and the so-called "Dallas contingent." Even the Latimer twins were present, having stayed on after their mother had left rather than return at the end of the month for Odelia's wedding. The staff hovered on the periphery of the room, including Carol, who held fast to Hunter's small hand. He shook free of her as Garrett and Jessa came through the door, and Garrett flashed him an encouraging smile, his heart swelling at this show of support.

"Well?" Ellie asked, coming forward to welcome her husband with a kiss.

"It isn't over," Magnolia announced, "but it's good."

Relieved sighs went around the room. Asher explained that not only would Garrett's parole not be violated, the dis-

trict attorney had agreed to support a motion of pardon on
Garrett's behalf, owing to the circumstances of his original
guilty plea and his obvious heroics in rescuing Hunter and
Jessa from her abusive ex. Garrett could still barely believe
it. Odelia squealed and leapt up to totter forward and hug
him, silver doves swinging from her earlobes. She'd decked
herself in every known peace symbol from praying hands
to love beads and wrapped her snowy head in a tie-dye scarf
that matched her skirt, which she wore with a bright yellow
blouse. Kent hauled himself up and waddled in her wake to
pound Garrett on the back.

"We have another wedding to plan!" Odelia rhapsodized,
clapping her hands.

"Oh, I think we'll do something very simple," Jessa said
quickly, basically confirming what had become common
knowledge.

Garrett squeezed her fingers, adding, "Simple and soon.
Maybe a small ceremony right here in the parlor with Pastor
Hub presiding." He looked to Hubner Chatam, who nodded
gravely.

"My pleasure."

Garrett wrapped his arm around Jessa's shoulders as Ellie
smiled up at her husband and said, "I highly recommend a
honeymoon in the Hill Country."

"What a nice wedding gift that would be," Hypatia suggested coyly.

Garrett didn't bother attempting to derail that generous
Chatam impulse. "I'd like a little vacation in the Texas Hill
Country," he said, looking to Jessa. "Wouldn't you?"

She nodded. "Billy and Abby can take care of things here
for a while." Olive had quit in confusion and embarrassment
when Jessa had explained that she had mistaken Garrett's actions and intentions.

"I'll help out, too," Magnolia volunteered, "so you can truly enjoy your vacation."

Hunter darted through the room to them, crying, "Oh, boy! Vacation!"

"Not you," Garrett told him gently, cupping his chin in one hand. "Not this time, buddy."

"Aw-w-w!" Hunter complained. Everyone laughed, and Garrett hugged him to his side to soften the blow.

"Maybe we can manage a family trip before school starts, though," he suggested. Hunter brightened only slightly.

Before Hunter could ask why he couldn't go, Chandler changed the subject, saying, "If you light out for Oklahoma, you won't have to wait." He and Bethany had eloped to Oklahoma when they'd wed.

"I think we can wait three days," Garrett said with a chuckle.

"Oh!" Jessa exclaimed, as if an idea had struck her suddenly. "We should've gotten our marriage license while we were at the courthouse!"

Garrett glanced quickly at his wristwatch. "It's not too late."

Asher produced a set of keys. "Take my car."

Garrett snatched the keys, laughing. They turned for the door, pausing as Hunter begged, "Can I come?"

Garrett glanced at Jessa, his heart swelling at the adoration in her eyes. Why would God bless him so richly? He thought his chest would explode with emotion. "Sure," he said to Hunter. "This time."

The three of them crossed the foyer and went out onto the porch. Asher's luxury SUV waited on the drive. It seemed to Garrett to be a symbol of the future, not that he cared a fig for luxury autos, but he'd been planning an economy-model life, and God, in His generosity, had provided too many upgrades to catalog.

"Did you ever dream it would come to this?" he asked Jessa.

"No," she answered, snuggling her head against his shoulder. "God has answered my every prayer with more generosity and abundance than I could even imagine. All I had to do was learn to trust. Him and you."

"Thank you," he whispered, bending to nuzzle her temple with his nose.

"Aren't we getting married?" Hunter asked, tugging impatiently on Garrett's hand.

Jessa laughed.

"Yes, we are," Garrett said firmly.

Hunter smiled so widely that the light reflected off his teeth. "Then what are we waiting for?" he demanded, breaking free to run to the vehicle.

"Not a thing," Garrett said, laughing and urging Jessa forward into the bright future. "Not a blooming thing."

* * * * *

Dear Reader,

Have you ever been wounded? We've all been wounded in some fashion. Usually it's emotional. Someone hurts our feelings. We may mope awhile, talk it out or even strike back. Eventually, though, we get over it and go on.

Some wounds are so deep and so lasting, however, that they affect our entire lives. We don't "get over it" so much as learn to go on in a different reality. We come up with all sorts of coping mechanisms: counseling, prayer, self-indulgence.... Only one thing truly brings healing, however.

Have you truly yielded your pain to God? It's tough to say, even to the One who suffered all pain to pay the sin debt of all people. "If You require this of me, so be it." Yet, that is the key to the joy that surpasses understanding, and we all have it in our hands. May you need it rarely but use it when you do.

God bless,

Arlene James

Questions for Discussion

1. The Chatam sisters do not believe in coincidence. Yet, the circumstances in which Jessa and Garrett find themselves seems entirely coincidental, each having arranged to lease the same property at about the same time from different owners. If not coincidence, however, what might it be?

2. Read Genesis 24. Do you see any similarities in Isaac and Rebekah's story and Garrett and Jessa's? If so, who would Magnolia be in Garrett and Jessa's version?

3. What reasons can you give for Hunter's shyness and silence? What other behaviors might he have adopted?

4. Garrett longed to see a toothy smile on Hunter's face and finally did so on the last page of the story. Why was that important to Garrett? What sort of emotion does that type of smile signify?

5. Despite the abuse that he had suffered at his father's hands, Hunter warmed up to Garrett long before his mother did. Are children more trusting than adults? Is this always a good thing? Why or why not? When is it a good thing?

6. Garrett's relationship with Magnolia Chatam was formed during his childhood and years later became the foundation of his chance at a life of freedom and meaning. Can you point to such a relationship in your life?

7. Garrett put off revealing the worst of his past to Jessa because he sensed that she would reject him because of it. Was this wise? Was it right? Did it become foolish or wrong at some point? Why?

8. Jessa had her own secrets. She had assumed her mother's maiden name in an attempt to hide from her abusive ex-husband. Was her secret as "wrong" as Garrett's? Why or why not?

9. Magnolia felt great regret and even anger at not being able to rescue Garrett from the situation that sent him to prison. Were her feelings justified? Why or why not?

10. All the evidence convinced Jessa that her wisest course was to keep away from Garrett. Yet, he seemed a great temptation to her. Was he a temptation? If the impulse to allow herself to trust him was not a temptation, what might it have been? Have you ever felt God urging you to do something against your better judgment?

11. Despite his violence and lack of trustworthiness, Jessa realized, shortly after arriving at Ellie and Asher's wedding, that Garrett did love her. What made her conclude that his feelings for her were genuine?

12. Both Garrett and Jessa had sought safe, "economy-model" lives. In the end, they felt that God had granted them "luxury-model" lives. Why would God do that? Was it a reward for past sufferings? Or was it a product of their ultimate faith in Him? Surrender to His will? Something else?

INSPIRATIONAL

Wholesome romances that touch the heart and soul.

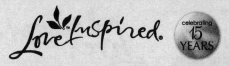

COMING NEXT MONTH
AVAILABLE FEBRUARY 28, 2012

LILAC WEDDING IN DRY CREEK
Return to Dry Creek
Janet Tronstad

DADDY LESSONS
Home to Hartley Creek
Carolyne Aarsen

TRIPLETS FIND A MOM
Annie Jones

A MAN TO TRUST
Carrie Turansky

HIGH COUNTRY HEARTS
Glynna Kaye

PICTURE PERFECT FAMILY
Renee Andrews

REQUEST YOUR FREE BOOKS!

2 FREE INSPIRATIONAL NOVELS
PLUS 2
FREE
MYSTERY GIFTS

LIREG11B

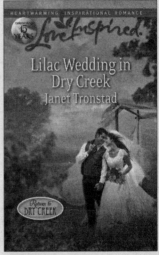

*When Cat Barker ran away from the juvenile home
she was raised in, she left her first love, Jake Stone.
Now Cat needs help, and she must turn to
her daughter's secret father.*

*Read on for a sneak peek of
LILAC WEDDING IN DRY CREEK
by Janet Tronstad.*

"Who's her father?" Jake's voice was low and impatient.

Cat took a quick breath. "I thought you knew. It's you."

"Me?" Jake turned to stare at her fully. She couldn't read his face. He'd gone pale. That much she could see.

She nodded and darted a look over at Lara. "I know she doesn't look like you, but I swear I wasn't with anyone else. Not after we—"

"Of course you weren't with anyone else," Jake said indignantly. "We were so tight there would have been no time to—" He lifted his hand to rub the back of his neck. "At least, I thought we were tight. Until you ran away.

"She's really mine?" he whispered, his voice husky once again.

Cat nodded. "She doesn't know. Although she doesn't take after you—her hair and everything—she's got your way of looking out at the world. I assumed someone on the staff at the youth home must have told you about her—"

His jaw tensed further at that.

"You think I wouldn't have moved heaven and earth to find you if I'd known you'd had my baby?" Jake's eyes flashed. "I tried to trace you. They said you didn't want to be found, so I finally accepted that. But if I'd known I had a daughter, I would have forced them to tell me where you were."

"But you've been sending me money. No letters. Just the money. Why would you do that? I thought it was like child support in your mind. That you wanted to be responsible even if you didn't want to be involved with us."

Jake shook his head. "I didn't know what to say. I thought the money spoke for itself. That you would write when you were ready. And I figured you could use food and things, so…"

"Charity?" she whispered, appalled. She'd never imagined that was what the envelopes of cash were about.

Jake lowered his eyes, but he didn't deny anything.

He had always been the first one to do what was right. But that didn't equal love. She knew that better than anyone, and she didn't want Lara to grow up feeling like she was a burden on someone.

Cat reminded herself that's why she had run away from Jake all those years ago. She'd known back then that he'd marry her for duty, but it wasn't enough.

Can Jake and Cat put the past behind them for the sake of their daughter?

Find out in LILAC WEDDING IN DRY CREEK by Janet Tronstad, available March 2012 from Love Inspired Books.